SONDER

DELILAH MOHAN

Chapter 1

WARREN

MY NOSTRILS WERE STILL BURNING from the scent of smoke. My lungs still fought to retract after being so close to the fire. You would think that a mutant who could breathe fire would be accustomed to such things, but the man trapped with the mutant was still just that, a man. A breathing creature. A half human; half lost, soul-searching for acceptance and equality.

"Relax," Ansel reassured me. "She's fine. She's with Rex."

He'd issued that reassurance many times before, so many times in the last twenty minutes that I wasn't sure who he was comforting. Me or himself. "I trust Rex. But I worry just the same. No one can protect our mate like I can."

"Calm the ego, Warren. We are all capable."

Only it wasn't an issue of ego. I felt the truth of it to my very core. I was the alpha. I was stronger. Faster. More capable than any being below me to protect our woman, and I wasn't close to her to do so.

The dirt and grime crunched under my boot, the sound echoing through the early morning. We were walking toward her apartment, and though I knew it wasn't far, it was still a walk I wish I didn't have to take. She defied me. The thought of her blatantly disobeying the orders I issued made the dragon rumble his displeasure. And even if her disobedience wasn't in question, I still felt off.

Something was wrong.

I knew it.

My stomach balled up, cramping uncomfortably. For a moment, I had to stop walking and hunch over, breathing through the pain.

"Something isn't right," I claimed when the pain finally eased enough that I could stand straight without flinching.

"Are they in danger?" Ansel's blank stare bore into me heavily.

"Any moment they aren't with me means danger." I gritted the words out through my teeth. "I protect what's mine."

My leaded feet moved forward; each step weighed down by the despair I felt inside. My dragon longed for his mate, and the absence of her when he wished to be close made him wallow in sorrow.

It would be fine, it had to be fine. Any other option was something I did not wish to entertain.

A sudden burst of pain followed by a wave of heat flashed over my body, and I swear my hair waved in movement, as if hot air pushed against me. My body relaxed, feeling sudden relief from a fire I hadn't even known was brewing.

"She's fine," I muttered, and fuck if I wasn't sounding

like Ansel. Fuck if I wasn't applying reverse psychology into thinking something that so clearly wasn't the case.

A turn onto the back alley had every hair on my body raise in warning. The smell of singed flesh and metallic blood filled the air, yet I saw nothing. I saw nothing, but I swear I felt it all. I swear my nerves were alive and receptive to everything I couldn't see, warning me of things I might not be ready to face.

The closer my feet took me to the fire escape, the more I knew. The more I dreaded. The more I had to force myself to take a step, one step at a time, until I reached my destination. At my back, I felt Ansel's presence, and I knew that if we were walking straight into danger, there was no person I'd rather have at my back.

"Do you want to split up?" he questioned as we moved closer.

It would be wise. It would be the absolute smartest decision if we were going to walk ourselves right into danger that we would do so from different directions, but I couldn't fathom splitting up in this moment from the only member of my family I still had my sight on. I needed him close because if I failed, I knew he would be at my back picking up the slack I could not control.

"We stay together," I stated as my hands gripped the metal of the fire escape.

"Together," he repeated the last word I spoke as my foot touched the first metal step, and it groaned under my weight. If I was going for stealth, I doubted I'd be able to accomplish it now. But if my mate was in danger, they would know I'd be coming. Stealth? Well, stealth wouldn't save them from me.

Each step I took heightened my anxiety. Each breath I inhaled tore and burned inside of me, forcing me to take in the scent of seared flesh and spilled blood. It grew the closer I got. The smell encouraged me to move faster even as my stomach wanted to pitch what little remanence it still had with the fear that something up in that apartment would ruin me. Would I be able to handle it? Could I handle my mate lying dead on a floor and not destroy this city from the pain of it?

The window was open when we reached it. The scent was nearly unbearable inside. Without entering, I could see the marks of a quick flame that filed out of the window, burning the brick and blackening the wall. I needed to enter, but I was panicked. Scared. Too damn timid over what I might see, and I couldn't bring myself to move forward.

"I hear nothing inside. No heartbeats. No threats," Ansel informed me as he approached my back.

"That should bring me comfort, but I only feel fear," I responded, before I closed my eyes and inhaled.

With little resistance, he pushed me aside. "I'll go then."

My hand shot up. "No. I'm the alpha. It's my job."

I didn't want to fucking go, but I couldn't wimp out and let him be braver than I was. It wasn't a question of my masculinity, for I was secure in that. But it was pride and honor. It was an honor as an alpha to take the first step into danger and protect those you love. If I shied away from that, I'd be a disgrace.

With a deep breath and all the nerves I could muster, I ducked my head and peered inside. The room was dark, but with the little light that the approaching dawn offered, I could see the bodies, lying charred and blackened, nearly melted into the flooring of Thea's former apartment. I closed my eyes, fighting the urge to vomit. None of them were her, I knew that. I could feel the truth in it. Still, the fear and logic warred inside of me, and I wasn't sure which one would win.

"Is it bad?"

I had forgotten for a moment that Ansel was there. The reminder urged me to stick a leg into the window and climb through. "It's not good."

"It doesn't smell good either," he muttered, and I had forgotten that whatever my senses gifted me regarding the scent, his gave him trifold. Fuck, to smell the aroma of death intensified was not a gift I wanted.

The ground crunched under my foot as I brought myself to my full height inside the room. My back straightened; my whole body tingled as I looked on. I tried to stifle the horror, but I couldn't. Not completely. I couldn't hide myself fully from my best friend.

"How many?" he asked.

I did a quick count of the bodies. All male, from what I could see. "Seven? Male. None is Thea."

Thank fuck for that. I should be worried, completely terrified that she wasn't here. But not having her body crisp on the floor at my feet meant she could be alive somewhere. Though judging by the drag marks that were embedded into the charred ground, I suspected I wouldn't be finding her back at our place. That thought made my dragon claw at my insides, trying to force his way out.

"Rex?" Ansel's voice was breathless.

The mention of Rex's name caused a fresh wave of panic to hit me. I had forgotten that Thea wasn't the only family I was missing. Rex was gone too, and I didn't want to check these men and discover if any of them were him.

"I can't…" I swallowed hard. "I can't tell."

"Warren," Ansel reasoned. "You need to focus."

"Thea is gone," I stated. It wasn't the only thing that mattered, but it was what my mutant wanted to focus on.

He wanted to be free. The claws he scrapped against my insides painfully were making it impossible to ignore. And I wanted him to be free. I wanted to release him into this world so it could numb me of the pain of her absence.

"Warren. Do you see Rex?" Ansel asked again and tried to focus my thoughts as I took a few steps around.

It was hard to recognize the bodies. The flesh was melted from the bones and what clothes they had on prior were burned into dust. The fire must have been intense and swift to tear through it all and fizzle out. A fire a beast such as my dragon could make.

I leaned over each lump of crispy human meat and tried not to be repulsed by the disgust of it. "I don't think he's here."

I made the statement after examining each one. None had his height. His build. His aura. As if I could actually see the aura of these bodies. But it felt off. None felt like him.

I looked around the space, noting two perfect circles of untouched ground. "There are two circles that the flames have not touched."

"Two?" Ansel questioned. "What blocked the fire?"

I…I didn't know. But if I allowed myself to truly dig, I could pull up a theory. I swallowed hard, allowing myself a moment of tormented peace before I spoke. "When we were walking, I felt discomfort."

"I remember."

"I felt fire burning inside of me," I clarified.

His body tensed near me. "Are you suggesting Thea did this?"

"I don't know what I'm suggesting," I admitted.

"It wouldn't be that crazy of a suggestion, Warren. We've seen how much she is becoming a part of us. Your fire could have been her last-ditch effort at protection, and from the smell of things, I wouldn't doubt that it was effective."

"It was. Too effective if the bodies and condition of this place had anything to do with it." My eyes roamed the room. "So, the clear untouched circles?"

"Probably held her and Rex inside." Ansel's assumption made sense. But—

"If they were the only ones who had lived, where are they now?"

I didn't expect him to answer. It was more of a question meant to walk me through what I've seen in front of me. Help myself piece together the atrociousness of what happened here. I bent down, picking up a dart that was on the edge of the circle, not burned by the flames.

"I found a dart." I handed it over to him, and he brought it to his nose.

"This would knock them out pretty good." He sniffed again. "It reeks of tranquilizers and sedatives. I don't think they would have made it far if they were hit with one or two of these. Add in a few more and it would have taken no time to make them crumble."

Rage consumed me, and for a moment, my vision blurred while dots danced along the edge. How dare someone sedate my mate? How brave of them to think they will live when I get a hold of them. They wouldn't. I'd make sure of that. I'd end their life painfully slow, taking joy in feeling their guts between my fingers and their blood ooze over my body. I'd bathe in it. Use it like fucking lotion to my moisten skin and sleep easy after knowing I had done the world a favor.

"They tranquilized my mate?" I asked through gritted teeth.

"Ours," he corrected before he brought the tip close to his nose and inhaled. His unseeing eyes closed tight as he shifted through the scents he was smelling. "It has her scent on the tip. This was in our mate's skin."

The roar that left me was uncontrollable. I was furious and there was no one near me to take out my anger on. My breathing picked up, the pants leaving my body rapidly as I fought through the rage.

Ignoring me, Ansel continued, "I don't think they just walked out of here themselves. There are only two circles, as you say, and this dart means that at least Thea was hit."

"There are also drag marks," I forced out the words through my panic.

"I think Thea released the fire she had absorbed from you, but those flames unknowingly protected Rex and herself. So either someone had to be on the outside, waiting, or Rex was already out and in this circle was the man who had activated the darts into their bodies."

"You think they carried Rex out?"

"I think they probably dropped him in favor of carrying her. But she would have protected him at all costs, and to lose control meant they were losing the fight. Rex probably was already out before they gained control."

My hands were damn near shaking at the thought of her in danger. "They snuck up on them." I looked up to see a single strand of string and a half-burned photo hanging from it. "They snuck up on them or distracted them enough that they wouldn't have seen it coming. They were both skilled. Rex would have never willingly allowed her to be harmed."

I reached for the chard photo and pulled it down. It held half a photo of a male's lower half, the head of the photo burned off and was a part of the surrounding ash. Ansel stepped closer, his feet crunching on the debris. "What did you find?"

"A burned photo hanging from the ceiling. This wasn't

here last time. If they put these all around, it's a big enough distraction for Thea to get thrown off."

"Were these photos——"

I cut him off. "I think the photos are of her kills. The marks they had assigned her. This image was a polaroid."

I rubbed the material in my fingers, feeling the film layers and melted plastic before handing it over to Ansel. He brought it up to his nose and sniffed, his nose crinkling. "That forced too much of crispy corpse into my nose. I may never get it out." He paused for a moment. "These weren't something from here. At least, they don't carry the scent I know as her apartment."

I stared at him, waiting for him to offer more. When he didn't, I asked, "What scent does it carry, Ansel? I need to find her."

My agitation was growing. Each second away from her was making it harder to keep the dragon inside, and I knew I shouldn't let him control me. I knew I was not one to go off emotions and, as an alpha, they expected me to maintain control of my feelings and do what I needed to for my people. But Thea was my mate, not my people. She was the main purpose I had for living. My very soul. And I had no clue where she was at.

"I'm not familiar," he admitted, but before I could explode with anger, he added, "But I'm going to get this to Rodrick as soon as possible. He might test it."

He tucked the photo into his front pocket, securing his promise, and fuck, I wished he could do more, but I guess the attempt at a solution was all I could ask for. I turned my back on him, stepping over the crispy bodies to make my way down the hall. It was untouched, flawlessly unaffected by whatever ignited in the living room, and it allowed me to walk unobstructed to her room.

Her room didn't seem out of order, minus the blanket

from her bed that sat in the hallway. Everything seemed in order. I went to the window, noting the large male footprint that was left on her window frame.

I would not shift.

I would not let the mutant rule over the man.

I would not lose my shit until I was positive Thea was around to bring me back from the brink of insanity.

But I wanted to. I wanted to lose all the fury I had and unleash it upon this world because she was gone, and I had no fucking clue where. I could track her. I knew this logically. But tracking took time, patience, the willingness to occasionally make the wrong turn, and when she was involved, I could not make a wrong turn. I would not allow myself to do so. The more wrong turns I make, the greater the chance of her ending up dead. And dead...

My heart beat frantically at the thought. Dead was not an option.

I walked back toward Ansel, picking up the blanket from the hall and bringing it to my nose. I inhaled deep. Thea. It smelled just like her. Her scent was embedded deep into the fabric, woven like thread into the material. My fingers flexed and fisted around the material, but I couldn't bring myself to release it, couldn't convince myself to let it fall to the floor and leave it behind when it was what seemed to be the only link I had to my mate at this moment. The only thing that was hers.

I took the blanket with me out to Ansel, clinging tightly to it for a moment more before I handed it to him. His body instantly relaxed. "There is nothing back there. It seems they came at them from both sides. There were footprints in her bedroom."

The thought of any man but me, Ansel, or Rex in her room made me furious.

"This her blanket?" He inhaled deeply. "The one you refused to let her retrieve."

Fuck. He was right.

If I had just gotten her this damn blanket, this whole thing could have been avoided.

"I'm not placing blame, Warren," Ansel interrupted my thoughts, catching up on to the direction they went. "Thea would have done whatever she wanted, regardless of the consequences. That fact has always been clear."

Still, I felt the guilt. Felt the weight of responsibility weighing me down. She was mine to protect, and I had failed at it. I had failed her.

"I don't think there is anything for us here. We'll go home." Without my mate. "And contact Rodrick for help." Ansel's demands seemed logical. Still, I hated prying myself away from the last place I knew she was.

I didn't want to agree with his suggestion, but it was the best possible solution for the time. "Home, then."

The words left my mouth, but I felt no attachment to them. Was it really a home without her there? In the time we'd known her, she had made the little cave that was carved into the underground feel more homely than it ever had in all the years of us living there.

I turned, my eyes traveling to the window we came in before halting on the vent on the floor. It wasn't fully pushed down, which seemed oddly out of place. Without speaking, I stepped closer, my head tilted in curiosity. When I was near, I dropped to my knees and leaned forward, grabbing a piece of paper that stopped the vent from closing.

It was a photo. One I'd never seen before, but instantly knew who it was. Her mother. The resemblance was unlike anything I'd ever seen. Her mother? A beauty like her daughter. And dead. The photo was grotesque in its taunts, teasing Thea with a life she hoped to one day reunite with, and this whole time, her mother had done the dance with death that we all so often prayed for.

I placed the photo into my pocket before threading my fingers into the grates of the vent and pulled it up. Blindly, not knowing what I was sticking my hand into, I reached into the hole, feeling around until I hit a solid book. Had Thea put it there? I gripped it, pulling it out, before checking for more. There was nothing else.

"I found a book in the vents and a photo of her mother. Dead."

"She had both?" he questioned.

But I knew deep down, she wouldn't keep a photo of her dead mother. "I think maybe the photo was left for her and fell into the space."

"And the book?"

I opened it, my mind suddenly whirling with photos, information, and oddly familiar codes, and then it clicked. I knew exactly why Thea had defied me, why she had put herself in danger. My throat was dry for a moment as I tried to speak. When I finally got the words out, they came out as croaked.

"The book? The book may be the key to breaking the computer program."

Chapter 2

THEA

MY HEAD POUNDED. My eyes burned. And as much as I wanted to open my eyes and look around, I physically couldn't. My whole body was on fire. Every limb felt stretched and abused and my mind, well, it was having a hard time connecting the dots as to why I felt like shit.

"She appears to be waking up." A voice funneled through my mind, sounding like it fought through a slurry of murk and mud to reach me.

"Should have hit her with one less dart." Another voice piped in.

Dart? They hit me with a dart? More than one? When? I couldn't remember a damn thing, though I searched my mind, trying to force memories that weren't there.

"She's a fighter. We've known this from the beginning. The extra dart was necessary."

If I chimed into this conversation, I would assure them that the extra dart was most definitely unnecessary. I felt like what I assumed an over boiled vegetable felt like, just lying limp and dull on whatever surface I was thrown onto. I raised an eyelid, barely, only to be assaulted with a bright stream of light. I slammed my eyelid closed, not ready to take the full blinding light head-on.

"Thea. Do you know why you're here?" I closed my eyes tightly, hating myself for giving away that I was lucid.

I licked my lips, cracked and dried. My throat, parched My mouth was gritty, and my tongue thick. It was like trying to speak after swallowing a desert. The only sound that escaped me was a desperate croak.

"Get her some water." In seconds, I had water drops slowly dripped into my mouth. I tried to lean into it, wanting more of it after the first drop hit my throat, but I couldn't move. The realization barreled into me hard. With that realization came the struggle and fight to be free; the struggle of knowing that I could not break these bindings, but I was going to die trying.

My arms pulled tight against the restraints, my legs trying to kick but unable to fight the ties. My back arched, the only thing not held down by ropes and chains, and though I wanted to shift my head to the side, wanted to turn it, the strap along my forehead hindered my movement.

"You won't get free, you might as well calm down." A voice to my left spoke, and I tried to see who spoke, but I failed.

I blinked my gritty eyes and swallowed hard, forcing back the bile that suddenly rose. When my words were spoken, they were hardly recognizable. "What do you want?"

The man closest to me, one I didn't recognize before, laughed. "Isn't it clear?"

If it was clear, I wouldn't have asked. Still, I bit my

tongue enough to rein in my sarcasm. I didn't want to provoke them, at least not yet. "Refresh my memory. My brain is a bit foggy."

He leaned over me, his face so close I could smell his rancid breath. "What better way for us to take down the dragon than to use his weakness against him?"

Take down the dragon? For a moment, I had no clue what that meant. Then, in a flash, it all came back to me, hitting me full force. A scream tore from my throat, shooting raw pain through my esophagus. The fight that I had stalled inside me came back with a vengeance as I struggled at the bounds that held me.

I refused to entertain the thought of what they wanted from me. I wouldn't do it. I wouldn't betray Warren. My heart hammered at the thought of his name, and with it, a flood of memories consumed my senses. My memories, my thoughts, the affections I held for him, Ansel, Rex.

Rex.

"Where's Rex?" I screamed. My voice sounded as panicked as I felt inside. He was with me. We were together. We had the best date of biscuits and gravy and then... then... my mind flashed to him lying in the hall of my apartment. His hands had trembled as he'd tried to stay lucid, but that fucking dart, those damn darts, had taken him out before he could defend himself.

And then... they got me, too.

Images filed in. My knife in a man's neck. My fight to gain control. Then Rex slumped over the shoulder of my former mentor, Jerome Kent. Darts, multiple darts, embedded in my skin. And the fire... the fire and the flames that had erupted from me and exploded throughout my apartment.

But that couldn't be real. That had to be a side effect of the darts and whatever sedative they carried because never in my life had I been able to call upon flames. Shadows. I could call upon the shadows and ask them to do my bidding, but never had I felt a power over fire.

Though, Warren can, and that thought alone made me uncomfortable. Had he been right this whole time? Was I completely theirs? So much so that I can use their power at will? I had seen things recently, things I tried to ignore... but never... never something this drastic.

"Where's Kent?"

If they would not tell me where Rex was, Kent would. He'd do it because every fucking person knows that in those vintage movies, the ones where the princess got caught by the villain, the villain loved to tell her his plan. Then her knight would sweep in and save the day. *Is Warren my knight?* Fuck no. But I believed he would come, and when he did, he'd be furious.

A furious Warren would not want to be someone I made enemies with.

"He's coming. Don't worry," a voice mocked. "As for your little lizard, why, he should be awake about now."

Little? There was nothing about Rex I'd consider little. His height was towering, his strength considerable, his tongue magical and his cock... well... let's just say Rex is a gifted mutant. He was gifted and his statute alone should be enough to intimidate these mediocre humans.

Somewhere beyond my visibility, a door opened with an audible release of a lock, then slammed closed. Footsteps walked slowly along the tile; each one growing closer to where I laid. Finally, Jerome Kent peered over me, his expression contemplative as he took me in.

"You're looking a little rough, sweetheart. Hard night?" He smirked at me, clearly aware of the exact reason I looked like I came off of a twenty-four-hour bender.

"Fuck you." I spat at him, taking satisfaction in the fact even though I was disorientated, I did not miss my mark.

He took out a handkerchief from his pocket and whipped his face. "Not happy with your amenities, I see."

Amenities? *Since when is being tied up and chained down on any list of amenities outside of a kink club? Unless this was his own personal kink club, in which case, where the fuck is the exit, because I would never, in my entire life, touch this man's dick.*

"Where is Rex?" I asked.

"The lizard is safe. I just had a brief visit with him. He's mighty furious that you aren't by his side."

"Take me to him," I demanded.

"Only if you're good."

"Good? I've never been good a day in my life."

"Oh, I'm aware. I practically raised you from a young teenager, training you, teaching you all you needed to know. All you needed to know, except the truth."

"The truth would have been helpful." I growled the words out.

"Don't worry about the little lizard of yours." He sighed. "You'll be reunited soon enough. Just some testing on the both of you, and into the holding cell you go. And I know what you're thinking, *is that smart?* By most standards, probably not. But you mutants, you give away so much unknowingly when you're together, and to be truthful, where we are putting you is the hardest room to get to. Warren, when he comes, if he is smart enough to find you, would have the hardest fucking time figuring out where his precious female is."

Did I not say the villain always talks? "What makes it so hard to get to?"

"You'll see," he muttered as a needle poked into my arm opposite of him. I tried to pull away, but I couldn't move my arm. This whole time, talking to him was a mere distraction so they could jab me with little resistance.

I forced my body to relax. There was no need for exerting energy when there was no way I'd break free of this. I lolled my head back toward him. "What are you doing to me?"

"Keep calm. It's just a little blood work. To start."

To start? "And then..."

"And then, well... we'll have to see what we find."

He shrugged his shoulders, like he didn't know exactly what type of torture I was about to be put into. It was a fucking lie. I knew it. He had a whole fucking grocery list of things planned for me, and I'd suffer through them, every fucking one of them, if it meant getting to Rex.

Chapter 3

REX

MY ENTIRE BODY ACHED. Mind, a fucking mess. And even through all the tests and procedures, lab work, and the fucking torture they used to get what the next move was out of me, all I could think of was Thea. Thea was my main objective. The only sole purpose of this life, and I refused, absolutely refused to give away anything that would hurt her.

I knew Warren wanted more. Warren wanted us to control it all, to grow as a family, to prove we were just as humane as the humans appeared to be, but my dreams were smaller. My dreams were the four of us and a lot of land in the middle of nowhere. Did we even need more?

When they asked, demanded, begged for me to give them information on the plans we had, I gave them none. My plans did not align with them, and if they didn't take living on a farmhouse in the middle of nowhere as a serious response, well, fuck them. Fuck every one of them because I had not a single doubt in my mind that I wouldn't get my dream, at least in partial.

They dragged my weak body down a dank hallway. This place had no windows, a fact that made me wonder just how far below the earth were they storing us. It would be a smart move to keep us below ground. It would give the others less of an access point. It would guard the public from viewing the chaos that would rain down upon them when Warren arrived. And he would. I knew that. There was nothing in this world that would guarantee these humans safety now that they had the life of his fully mated mate in their facility.

This place will fall in flames, with the humans begging for forgiveness on their knees.

"I thought these freaks were stronger than this," the douche, who dragged one side of my body, stated. "This one is as weak as a new fawn. Can't even get his balance."

"If you wanted strong, you should have snagged one of the others." I grunted the words out as they handled me like a rotten bag of potatoes. I wasn't the strong one, and I did feel as weak as a fawn if I was honest. In the time at this facility, I'd had things injected into me, multiple rounds of blood work, scans, been cut open, sewn closed, and that was all before the beatings for information. The delicious biscuits and gravy I had enjoyed so much had long since left my body, ejected from me sometime between the third and fourth mystery injection. So yeah, I was a fucking weak-ass bastard right now.

But being weak didn't mean I had no desire to kill them.

Their life was a ticking time bomb, and at any moment, it would detonate.

They pulled open a door to a stairwell, and instead of giving me the option to walk, they pushed me down, laughing hysterically as I hit the stairs and fucking rolled to the bottom. My fury surfaced, but I wouldn't act on it. Not yet. I'd save my energy for when I knew the others were near. I reached out, my hand finding the rough edges of a brick wall. Digging my fingers into it, gripping it as tight as possible, I pulled my body upward. I gritted my teeth against the pain while I closed my eyes, trying to fight against the blackness that was creeping in.

The guards' footsteps pounded against the steps as their laughs died down. A foot greeted my vision. Fingers grabbed into my arm, giving me no warning or a chance to catch my balance as he pulled me away from the support of the wall. I stumbled forward, hardly getting my feet under me before the next set of hands grabbed onto my other bicep.

"What type of mutant are you again?" A laugh sounded as my foot caught against the floor, dragging behind me, twisting my body in an awkward position. "A tiny little kitten?"

"I can play any type you want as long as you know that when you're begging for your life, it won't be a kitten coming at you."

An elbow hit my face, and I jerked my head to the side before spitting out a mouthful of blood. They didn't like that. They didn't like being told that their end was near when they were so confident that they would come out in a superior position. Only I knew what Warren was capable of. They had only heard rumors. Rumors that never fully captured his full potential. Rumors don't talk about the fear in the eyes of the people he kills, or the brutality of their blood coating the walls and the surface nearby. They'd find out on their own, and I hoped I'd be there to see it.

They hit a few numbers on a pin pad and a door popped open. "Ready to see your bitch?"

The words sent a jolt of rage through me, and I couldn't help but rebel, tripping them as they walked beside me. The jolt of pain as a fist slammed into my spine was worth it, even as I doubled over, and my stomach rolled from the pain of it. They forced me to keep walking, to move through the pain until they reached a door. A heavy ring of keys surfaced from one of their pockets, and they placed the key inside, unlocking it. The door groaned as they pulled it open, and before I realized what was happening, they pushed me inside.

I fell hard to my knees, lucky my hands braced automatically in front of me, saving my face from smashing to the cement floor. Behind me, the door slammed shut, hard enough to shake the windowpane on it. I gritted my teeth and inhaled, before crawling to the wall and using it as a support to force myself up. My legs almost gave way, my body struggling against gravity as it tried to pull me down. Fighting the dizziness, I took a step toward the door, and then another until I was no longer in front of a wall, but in front of the window on the entrance.

The window was tiny, maybe a square foot, but it allowed me just enough room to see outside. The place we had walked to was nondescript. Gray brick, gray cement flooring, and if I strained hard enough, I thought I saw a thin white painted line along the boring wall. But there was absolutely nothing that gave away where we were. Nothing to tell me how close Thea was to me or if I'll see her again. Nothing to tell me the time or date, or give me any indication of just how long I'd been in this manmade hell.

I sunk to my knees, trying not to feel the overwhelmingness of despair. There was an end to this. I knew that for certain. They wouldn't kill us. They needed us. They needed both Thea and me to draw in the dragon, and if either of us weren't here when he arrived; they knew his rage might be uncontainable. We were the bait. They didn't take into account Warren's rage would be inhumane, regardless. There would be no stopping it. There would be no survivors. Each time he transforms into his dragon, it becomes more intense, more bloody, more of a challenge to keep him and his powers contained.

They'd better hope that even after they had taken his mate; he remained a man. After all, their lives depended on it.

I slunk down against the furthest wall of the small room. The cold brick against my skin served as a reminder that the situation I was in left me completely fucked. My stomach growled, reminding me it had been empty of contents long ago, and I doubted we would get the luxury of a solid meal in this place. I took in the dimly lit space. There was nothing here but walls, floor, and a bucket in the corner.

Used for… animals.

They treated us like animals while expecting the respect one would give their equals.

We were not their equals. Maybe once before they had decided their superiority. Now? We were their superiors; a fact only encouraged and brought on by their dislike of our differences. Warren had been right this whole time. If we don't take control and make change, change will never come. Not at the hands of the ordinary humans who want so fucking bad to be something as special as us.

I let my head fall back against the wall, and I drifted. For who knows how fucking long until an obnoxiously loud beep in the hallway stole away my sleep. My eyes fluttered as I tried to force them open with resistance. I shook my head, gaining lucidity before I laid my hand on the wall, forcing myself to stand. Letting go of the stability, I walked toward the window on the door to peer out.

Thea.

My heart beat frantically as she got closer.

She looked drained of energy, but not beat up like me. Her hands were tied behind her back, and judging by the glare she wore, I suspected that was a recent development in my feisty mate's attire. What had she done to them? I didn't doubt that she caused a whole slew of unnecessary events because she was a fighter, forced to be by circumstance, and she wouldn't let them have the upper hand.

I clung to the door, my hands pounding against the metal, though I knew it was so thick, she couldn't hear a single noise. She got closer and my blood pumped through my body so fast that I could hear it in my ears. They wouldn't put us together. Would they? We couldn't be so lucky. Except...

They stopped in front of the door. Her four guards flanked her as one used a key to open the cell door. I stepped back, schooling my face to neutral. I didn't want them to know I was excited about the possibility of her being with me. If they knew, they would take her from me, and I needed to check over her. I needed to find out if she was okay. I needed to nuzzle myself into her neck and make sure they hadn't hurt her.

The door popped open, and before she could enter, two of her guards rushed me, forcing me back against the wall. I would not hurt them, not if it meant risking Thea. They forced my hands up above my head as they wrapped my wrists in chains. I didn't fight them. Not when they looped the chains into rings on the wall and wrapped it around my neck. I couldn't move... I didn't dare try. I'd suffer through the chains if it meant having my mate close to me.

Securing the chains with a thick lock, they stood back. With a flick of a hand, they gestured for Thea to be brought in. With her, they didn't hesitate to remove her chains. They fell from her wrists to the ground, and she shook out her hands, glaring.

A throat cleared. "Don't fucking try anything else. We'll bring you food shortly."

Food? The thought had my stomach growling, but I wouldn't get my hopes up. They pushed Thea forward, causing her to stumble before stepping back, not taking their eyes off of her until they were at the door. The door slammed, the impact shaking the floor. She waited until she heard the lock click shut before she rushed toward where I sat on the cement.

Thea fell to her knees in front of me and, for the first time in what seemed like a lifetime of existence, I got to look into her eyes again. The blue wasn't nearly as vibrant as it was when she was free, but still; it comforted me. Her hands touched my face, stroking over the bruises and broken skin. "They will pay for this, Rex. I promise they will."

I tried to lean toward her. The chains dug into my neck so tight that I nearly choked. I fell back, swallowing hard. "Did they hurt you?"

"Not nearly as much as I hurt them." She smirked, and I didn't doubt that to be true for a single second. "Nothing as bad as what they did to you. What happened?"

I shrugged, the chains rattling with the movement. "They wanted to know Warren's plan."

"After a few questions, they assumed Warren didn't tell a female such things. Fuckers. Those goddamn sexist bastards."

The way she fumed was so damn cute. "Did you expect anything less than that, Doe?"

"I'll put a knife through every one of their hearts for this. I swear it." She gritted her teeth, and her hand searched my body for damage.

"I'm thinking you like us, Doe. What do your shadows think about that?" I leaned as far into her touch as I could, savoring the comfort it brought me.

She sighed and pulled back some. "I don't like you. The shadows though, they've always liked you. Warren is different. He's..."

"Addicting," I cut in, and even though I was smiling, she was glaring.

"I was going to say infuriating, but that's also true." Her head turned toward the door. "He will come, won't he?"

"For you? He'd climb to the sun if it meant saving you."

Her eyes were serious when she said, "For the both of us."

I knew she was right. Warren would come for me. We were family. But the urgency of my rescue versus hers was vastly different. She was his mate; I was his best friend. One of those, no matter how much she tried to deny it, trumped the other. I swallowed the lump in my throat, the one that formed every time I thought about her being our mate. "You didn't use your shadows in here, did you?"

"No." Her eyes were so beautiful when they were focused on me alone, and I hated I couldn't just reach forward and grab her. I tried, though. I strained my arms against the metal, pulling it tight against my wrist, which then pulled the chain against my throat. Those mother-fuckers. They needn't have put me in chains, but it was for their own amusement. She licked her lips, and my eyes followed. "I knew better than that. Under observation, using my ability was exactly what they were hoping for."

"Same here," I assured her. "They are curious, but they

won't admit it. They want to know exactly what we can do and how we've grown just as much as they want us all eliminated."

"It's fear driven. They really fear our strength. They should. If we all unleashed what we were capable of, we could do great things."

"Amazing, extraordinary things." I agreed because in this situation, we were the bad guys. We'd kill, murder, and slay anything in our path in order to get what we want. But what we want was for a good cause. We were good people doing shit things in order to improve the life of everyone. We may be painted as the villains, but we were the saviors.

"We are their leverage, you know that, right? That if they didn't need Warren, they wouldn't keep us alive."

I knew in my mind that this was true. "If we didn't have Warren, you would be blissfully unaware that we existed and still out being stabby, stabby at their command."

"This is true." We heard the loud, obnoxious beep in the hall sound again, and she paused, distracted. "Though I would like to point out, it was a little more complicated than feeling stabby. What do you think they want with Warren?"

What they wanted with Warren was a loaded question. She didn't know his whole backstory, and it wasn't my job to tell her. It was Warren's, and though this quest for me and most of us was for the good of everyone, Warren's quest was more personal. The president wasn't just a target to take down; it was his primary target. His enemy from the moment he took his first breath as a mutant. Their past had led to this point and it could have been different, should have been, if only mutants were treated as equals and not as abominations.

The door scraped, and we turned that direction. With

a groan, the door was pushed open, and a tray of food was pushed in. Without a single word, the door slammed shut again. We stayed silent for a moment, not daring to breathe as we waited for anything that might disturb us. When nothing came and no other man opened and entered, she crawled forward, grabbed the tray with one hand and pulled it back toward us. The smell of food hit, and my mouth instantly watered. Bread and some type of watery soup. It would do.

My stomach growled, and Thea smirked. "Hungry?"

"Starved." Though I wasn't just referring to food. She was an addiction and just seeing her again caused my blood to warm until it was past the point of simmering and my cock to stand at attention.

She tore off a chunk of bread and held it up. I opened my mouth, fucking hating the circumstances but loving the opportunity they had offered me. She pushed the bread into my mouth and my lips closed around it, catching her finger. I sucked on it for a moment before letting it release. She raised a brow. "I suddenly have a feeling that our star-vations have vastly different meanings."

I chewed the chunk of bread slowly before swallowing it. "Yeah?"

"Yeah." She smirked before she stirred the pitiful soup. "This is... well... Enjoy."

She scooped up a spoonful of broth with the smallest chopped piece of some sort of vegetable and held it up to feed me. I would not deny myself of this substance. My mouth opened, and she shoveled it in before she took her own bite. "Delicious, right?"

She gave me a side-eyed glare before grabbing a piece of bread for herself. "It's nothing like that Mac and cheese that stupid guard was eating ten minutes before dragging me down here."

The thought of macaroni and cheese was enticing. "An unorthodox form of torture, but it still is effective."

She offered me a bite of bread. "Want to know what else is an unorthodox form of torture?"

I chewed slowly on the piece, trying not to choke on the stale crust. "What?"

A slow smile formed before her eyes drifted lower on my body. "You'll see."

Chapter 4

ANSEL

MY HEART HAD BEEN in an overdrive ever since the diner, and even though I constantly reassured Warren that everything was going to be alright, I knew in my gut that it most definitely wasn't. I trusted Thea. I trusted Rex. But what I didn't trust was the United government or the fact that they wanted our heads on a platter and our bodies sliced open for their own scientific reasoning.

I'd smelled the charred, burned flesh before we even approached, and I knew it was bad. How bad? Well, I didn't expect the body count lying on the floor of Thea's former apartment to be as high as Warren had counted. But I was so fucking thankful Thea or Rex weren't part of the deteriorated bodies laid out on display.

Not being one of the bodies, though? That only meant they were a victim of a different level. A bait to lure Warren into a trap, to bring him forward so that they may toss their heavy weighted nets upon him and fill his body with so much sedative that even an enormous elephant wouldn't survive.

I had thought Warren would break. He damn well seemed close to it. But he held strong, letting the logic and strength of an Alpha rule over his emotions, barely. I had felt the moments within him, felt the subtle shift in the surrounding atmosphere, the slight dip of temperature that showed that maintaining control was a struggle for him. It was a battle between himself and the outside world, and if he let himself gain control, the outside world would suffer.

"Are you clinging to a blanket?" Rodrick asked the moment he stepped into Warren's office. He had traveled to us, bringing a small team with him. It was wise. The state of Warren's mental well-being was fragile, and the slightest shift could cause Rodrick's community more damage than he already caused when our omega went into heat.

Warren growled; his words spoken through gritted teeth. "It's Thea's and I'm not clinging to it. I'm just holding it."

I knew he was clinging. He hadn't put it down since we left the damn apartment. "Did you bring the equipment needed?"

I cut into the conversation, drawing the attention away from Warren and the omega's blanket. Rodrick cleared his throat. His voice projected my direction. "Yeah. They are bringing it in now. It will take some time. It's a long trek from our entrance point through these tunnels."

"Understood." I put my hands down on the desk, feeling around for the book Thea had left in the vent of her apartment. "This is what we have. Warren says it's familiar."

Rodrick grabbed the book that I offered him. The pages crinkled as he turned them, skimming the book's content. "I don't know why I hadn't thought to cross-refer these."

"So it's useful?"

"I...I think so." There was a pause in the room. "I won't know for sure until I'm into the system again and I can begin decoding, but I think this would help."

"And my mate?" Warren cut into the conversation that revolved around the government, reminding us what was important.

"We'll find her," Rodrick reassured him. "Have you tracked her?"

"I was waiting to do so. Thea is my priority, but not my only one. I needed my city protected." He paused, sniffing the air. "Her scent is still strong. I can track her, but I think it would be easier to locate possible facilities first. If I know what facilities are in the area or the direction, that could limit the time spent."

When had Warren become so logical? Oh yeah, he was always logical, just not in Thea's presence.

"You sure you don't want to go after her immediately? I've never had a mate before, but from what I know..."

"I'll wait," Warren interjected. "She is the bait. They have time to prepare for me, but I haven't had time to prepare for what I might face. They won't kill her; about that, I'm positive. At least not until they have me. I am what they want."

"After that show in the apartment, the combustion she showed, I suspect they might be a little more interested in her now," I added, before directing my question at Rodrick. "Have you been to her apartment yet?"

"No." The book hit the wood of the desk as he placed it down. "But I have men breaking into camera streams of local CCTVs and we are sending in a nondescriptive air camera to get footage. I'd like to see what happened and maybe get some info. I'll send a rover later to get some samples."

A rover was a small robotic that Rodrick created just for this purpose. It could enter a place that wasn't deemed safe for us, get the material needed, then slide out. If spotted, Rodrick, who was controlling it through a camera, could hide, lose the tail, or in a worst-case scenario, self-destruct. It was smart to use one in this circumstance. It had already been proven that Thea's apartment was under the eyes of the government, and if they were watching, they probably already knew Warren was there. Their next step would be to collect their dead and do a cover up to pretend like none of this had happened.

"I hadn't thought about camera footage." Warren tapped a pen against the desk. He may not have thought about it, but I had. Only for me, cameras did no good. Their importance was not a priority on my list of evidence review tools when I couldn't observe what was going on. "It might help to see if we recognize any of the team? That might direct us to possible locations as well." There was a pause. "And it will allow us to see the condition of my beta and my omega as they left."

I knew of the condition of them. Out like a fucking light. There was no passable way unless she was uncon-scious. She was a fighter. Strong, brave, beautiful, if anything I pictured in my mind had any validity in it. Not a single man or mutant could touch her without her blade piercing their skin. If they got the upper hand, especially after the condition of her apartment, it was because she could not stop it. But that apartment proved well enough that she fought with every ounce of her being.

"I'll have that information prioritized," Rodrick added, before gathering his thoughts. "About the main mission. I-I didn't know Luis was dirty. I had no indication. I trusted him."

I could feel his words to my core and I knew he spoke the truth. He never would put us in danger. We had known Rodrick since we were kids. Our lives meant more to him than most things. Betraying us and putting us in danger served no purpose. Warren understood that too when he said, "It's taken care of."

"Good." Rodrick's voice raised with a touch of laughter. "So is my property damage."

Fuck, an omega in heat, slick and wanting for us, was a fucking occasion I hoped to repeat. I didn't care whose property it damaged. I was about to open my mouth, remark something along that thought, when my mind suddenly latched on to the thought of an omega. "There is something else."

Rodrick's hand slapped the wood. "Of course, there is something else. There is always fucking something else with you guys."

"We had gone to the diner before we went to the apartment. They burned it down. A witness put Thea and Rex there and then confirmed that shortly after they were robbed, a girl was kidnapped, and the place was torched." As if I was traveling back, my nose twitched from the scent of smoke.

"Why is this important?" Rodrick seemed impatient, as if he knew the ball was about to drop and he didn't want to wait for it to happen.

"It's important." Warren's voice boomed. "Because that girl was Thea's friend. She was Thea's friend and an omega."

"Another omega?" Rodrick seemed in awe. We knew they were out there. He shouldn't be shocked. Still, finding Thea was a miracle. Learning that there was another right here the whole time? Well, I guess I understood his amazement.

"They didn't kill her," Warren proceeded. "This supports what we had wondered. If they abducted her, how many more do they have? Could that be the reason it had been so hard to find mates?"

Nothing shocked me. The government had already gone through great lengths to make us suffer. A little more suffering at the hands of them by preventing procreation and stopping new life? It was not that farfetched. If they were keeping them, though, it meant they had plans for them. They were using them somehow, and that thought was terrifying.

"I'm going to the diner site," Rodrick announced.

"You'll have to wait. It's crawling with law personnel." Warren took a deep breath. "Tell me my mate is all right? That nothing bad will become of her when I'm not there."

Rodrick hesitated. He didn't want to promise safety and security when we didn't have eyes on her. "She will be fine. That beta... let's hope he watches his mouth."

A real worry for Rodrick because he and Rex were close, and a loss like that, well, he'd feel it hard.

"Impossible," I joked to lighten the mood.

"I know," Rodrick continued. "That's what I'm afraid of."

Chapter 5

WARREN

I WAS SLOWING GOING INSANE. I knew it. I could feel my mind wander in whatever direction it picked, thinking of all the scenarios that could play out right now, and I was fucking ready to lose all hold I had on reality. Logically, I know it was me they wanted, not my sweet little Doe, but I had no room in my life for logic. Not now. Not fucking ever. Not when Thea was involved.

I wished Rodrick worked a little fucking faster. The moment I called him, I already regretted it. Calling and agreeing to wait in place meant I couldn't be halfway out of the city already searching for her, following her scent to the nearest location and causing destruction. But as Rodrick reminded me, as he had already guessed my train of thought, distraction wasn't our goal. Life preservation was, even if those lines were the lives of the basic individuals who were yet to support us. We didn't want to off the civilians of the world, but I would be lying if I didn't say that in this moment, nothing would cause me greater joy.

I peered over Rodrick's shoulder, keeping my eye on the screen as he typed away. He didn't even turn toward me. "Calm down."

"Easy for you to say. It's my fucking mate." He didn't understand. He'd not been mated. Hadn't felt the indescribable, soul-wrenching pain of having her torn away from him unwillingly.

"These notes she left... she's thorough." He was looking at the folder I had dug from the vent. He had no clue just how thorough my girl was. Thorough in every fucking way that counted.

"What do you have?"

"I think I've found a correlation between these and the key we were trying to break. It appears the numbers of these ... victims' identities... all have a similar theme. The last number of their identities seems to correspond with a reasoning. Like these three here..." He took out a few files and laid them in front of me. Familiar faces, even if I had known little about them personally. "These were all mutants who held semi powerful jobs. It kept up the appearance of the society for a while, but now that they are trying to eliminate us, it doesn't matter."

"The appearance was no longer needed." I mused. "And the rest of the numbers?"

"I'm still working on it. However, the first set of numbers seems to have to do with locations. If you notice here"—he pointed to various files—"they were all killed in Valley Springs." He grabbed another set of files with different numbers that all seemed to match. "And here? Here they were all killed in the Gilded Heights."

"All where large government buildings are of operation," I stated the obvious.

"Exactly. I'll try to decode the rest of them, but so far, I've only gotten a handful. But Thea only worked local. If they have taken her further, the code might not be in this set."

"But you can use them to break the codes that aren't, right?"

"I'm entering the data into my programs now."

"I'll wait." As if I had a fucking choice. My mind was already screaming for my mate. I was ready to hit the streets on foot and sniff her out until I found her. I didn't care how far I had to go; I'd find her. But... finding her on foot would take long. Finding her using the information that the system offers? A little less, hopefully.

I forced myself to stop hovering. I trusted Rodrick, his team—the men he kept at his back with my life, and when the time came, if I needed them to be at mine, I knew without a doubt they would be there for me. My feet carried me outside of my office and down the stone path that led to our home. Our little slice of heaven cut out into the cavern wall, with a single curtain dividing us from the rest of the world we had single-handedly created.

I'd get her better. My mate deserved better. She deserved a palace on a mountain top, not a hole in a cave wall. Though she never complained about the accommodations, I knew that if she belonged to me, she would get the very best from here on out. And she belonged to me. She may fight the admission, but the truth was so clearly obvious. She. Was. Mine.

"You up?" I asked as I pushed aside the curtain. Ansel had left the room long ago, and since I knew Rodrick had it under control, I needed to search out Ansel. I needed my family close. I needed the reassurance that together, we would get through this and find her.

"Like I could sleep." He was sitting in a chair. "This is going to be a setup, you realize that?"

"You know I do."

"But I mean, to what extent of it?" He paused as he stared straight ahead, never at me, even when he was look-ing. "It could be a massacre again."

"I would be shocked if it wouldn't be."

"If your dragon comes out to play again—"

"My dragon will come out when he absolutely needs to. He would do anything to protect her. I think we've all real-ized that right now. And if… if she… if—" Shit, I couldn't even voice the main concern. We just spent a solid four days fucking, mating, insinuating. She may not have real-ized what that meant or might mean, but fuck it. We all did. I dropped my train of thought at that. Ansel would know what I meant. "We would protect her regardless of the circumstances of our life."

End of story.

Final statement.

Nothing would stop me.

Thea is mine and what's mine is protected.

"I trust you both, Warren." He sighed. "I didn't mean offense. I just… I don't know. I just worry that if he forces his way out again, I may never see my best friend again. We don't need your dragon to protect her. Rex and I, and you even, combined, are enough to keep her safe and, if you've forgotten, our omega is not a damsel in distress. She's powerful, strong, so fucking ruthless that it makes my stomach tighten."

"Tighten?" He questioned. "Really? It just makes my cock hard."

Her resistance made me shiver. Her mouth made me lust. Her knife at my throat damn near made me come on the spot. Everything about her feisty ways turned me on, and I'd fucking die before I lost it. I'd lie down at the feet of my enemy before I let them take the most important to me, and I was forced to watch her perish inches away. Power was nice. It was a fucking luxury, but I'd pick Thea over any power any day.

I should go to her.

I should ditch this plan to find her location and just fucking go find my mate.

I needed to.

I needed to be close so fucking bad that my skin itched and crawled, and I had to clench my fingers into fists to prevent myself from barreling out of the tunnel. But this situation needed wisdom. Strength. Force. And fuck, I hated that I'd to use all those traits on myself just to maintain any sort of control, when all I wanted to do was fucking lose it and unleash it into the world. The world would burn. The fury I felt bubbling inside of my stomach would hit all around me like molten lava, and there would be no protecting it from my wrath.

"Control yourself." Ansel's voice broke into my thoughts, and I looked toward him. He appeared casual, but I knew he was anything but. "We will find her. I can smell the room filling with smoke and all indicates that the source is you."

Was I smoking in my silent, seething rage? I hadn't noticed.

"I can't help it."

"You can. Learn to fucking control yourself, Warren. If we're going to save our family, you need all the control you can fucking get. Last time, in the government building, you lost your shit, and yeah, you protected her, but it almost cost us our lives."

He was right, but I didn't want to admit it. "It didn't. I saved us."

"Barely." He glared at me, his eyes not bothering to blink, and for a moment, I thought he really could see me standing here. "We barely made it, Warren. And if Thea hadn't been able to bring you back from the edge, it would have been a fucking catastrophe. We do not want a repeat, do you understand?"

Being scolded by my delta felt off. I was the one in charge, yet here he was, commanding me. I wasn't a child. I was the alpha. And being the alpha meant, well, it meant Ansel was fucking right. I needed to keep my shit together for fear that I would risk them all. "No repeats."

"Whatever the plans, we figure them out together," he said.

"Together it is."

"You are not alone on this," he stated as if he needed to reassure me. Was that even his job? Shouldn't I reassure him? "You need to trust that Thea is capable."

"I know she is capable."

"Do you?" He quirked a brow. "Because sometimes it seems you've forgotten that before we were with Thea, she was slaughtering full-grown mutants. She is magnificent in the darkness, Warren, don't forget that. But in the light, with a blade in her hand, she's a fucking masterpiece."

She is a masterpiece.

My fucking masterpiece.

I closed my eyes and inhaled, slowly exhaling and releasing tension. He was right. Thea could stay alive, and Rex was capable of doing the same. I was worried. Terrified. But I had to go about this the logical way. We had to be prepared. Going in half-ass wouldn't help any of us if we got captured.

"We're going to have to expedite our plans for a takeover."

Ansel rubbed the heel of his palm into his eyes. "I was afraid of that, too."

"There is no other choice. Go big or go home." I didn't want to go home. Not until this whole fucking country was considered my home; not a tiny slice of underground that I carved out for safety.

"Let's not go home until we've got what we wanted." Ansel leaned forward, using his knees to prop up his elbow. "I don't know where she is. But wherever she is at, we get her. Then we go straight for the capital. They won't expect such rapid concession of actions."

"The amount of risk involved in moving from one to the other is..." I didn't want to speak the words into existence.

"Our key priority is our family. We can always abort if needed," he assured me, but I hoped it didn't come to that. We could abort. That was true. But by aborting, we lose an element of surprise. We needed that element in order to prove that they couldn't stay one step ahead of the mutants forever. That we were determined to be seen and be heard, and we were fucking people just like them.

"If it means risking Thea, we will abort. Otherwise, I am confident we have the support we need."

Footsteps thumped against the stone, and we froze, alert and ready to strike if needed. The steps grew closer, and my heart raced. Having someone approach my personal residence was new. No one ever came this way, and I liked that about the location. It was private. Secretive. Mine. Ours, my family's.

A knuckle knocked against the stone, and my nerves jittered. "Yeah?"

Rodrick cleared his throat. "I've got something."

I stepped forward, pushing open the curtain so that we were eye to eye, staring at each other. "What?"

"Project Greek Island."

I blinked a few times, not understanding the complete rubbish that was spoken to me. "Excuse me?"

"Project Greek Island," Ansel repeated. "I thought that place was long gone." He swallowed hard. "Thea's in Virginia."

Chapter 6

THEA

THE AUDACITY HAD ME FUMING. That they could wrap a chain around Rex's neck and treat him like he was cattle while I, the same girl who attacked them in the hall, had nothing binding her. Why was that? I suspected they knew that if Warren saw me in bindings, there would be no way to control his rage. Little did they know no one would ever control a beast like Warren. They might lessen the rage, but the rage would still simmer just under the surface, and it would be released.

I ran my fingers under the chain at his neck. "Does it hurt?"

Rex closed his eyes against my touch, leaning into my hand slightly. "Only when I pull at it."

"And your arms?"

"Fucking dead at this point." I looked up to where his hands hung limply from his bent wrists. The color wasn't nearly as vibrant as they normally were, and fuck, this whole thing made me furious. It was my fucking fault. It was my fault we were in danger because I had to go back to my apartment. I had to defy Warren's orders, and sure, the reason was partially out of needing the information, but the other part? Pure spite. I could admit it. I knew Warren would be furious if he found out, and now? Well, fuck, now he knows.

The obnoxious buzz rang through the room, and I jumped away from Rex, plastering my back against the wall. I knew they were coming for us, or because of us, and I wasn't scared. Nothing truly scared me under most circumstances, but I wanted to be far away as possible. I reached my hand over, my fingers squeezing his thigh before I pulled away.

"It will be fine, Thea. They won't kill us."

He was so confident. Always. And though I knew they wouldn't kill me, I was the fucking bait. Did they really need Rex by my side? Did he serve a purpose for being here, or was he here to keep me in line? If that was why they kept him around, it would work. I didn't want to do a damn thing to jeopardize him. Now that I had him so close to me, I'd cooperate.

The keys in the door clanked heavily, and my fingers flexed with tension as I waited to see what was happening, what did they want, what was their fucking plan. It opened slowly as they waited, suspecting we'd attack. We wouldn't. Not when Rex was at risk. Not when my body was just having the effects wear off from the dart and I was feeling like myself. To test, I pulled at a shadow and it moved toward me, lurking and trudging at a slower pace than normal, but still, it had moved. It was there if we needed the protecting.

The door hit hard against the wall before multiple men stepped in. I smirked. "You afraid of a weaponless female and her chained companion?"

A man reached down and grabbed our tray of dishes. The food was pitiful, but it gave me a little more energy, and if we needed to fight right now, we'd do it.

A man stepped out from the group, taking on the leader's role. "Afraid of a weaponless female? No. Afraid of a mutant who is a trained assassin and can combust, yeah. Slightly. But don't you worry, little roach, we've got you handled now."

Did they think so?

Maybe for the time being, but there was no way they would permanently control me. I looked over at Rex, his body beaten and broken by cuts and bruises. No, they couldn't control me forever, not when retribution screamed to be taken for the wrong they had done to my mate. My fucking mate. Ownership coursed through me, urging me to take action now, but I knew I had to wait. I couldn't act rashly until I knew Rex and I had the support for a backup.

"You can remove his chains."

"We could, but we won't. How stupid would we have to be to let two mutants be free? Him? He will be a casualty in our war against mutants. We can't harm you too much because the mutant who is obsessed with you would destroy us all. We are aware. We can't kill you until he's fully dead, sadly. But no one cares about a lowly reptile."

Lies. I cared about that reptile. Warren cared about that reptile. Rex, Rodrick... we all fucking cared, and he wouldn't be hurt. "You think it's only me that Warren would destroy the universe for? Then you don't understand our family very well."

"Family? You're all a bunch of orphan freaks. Hardly a family. Hardly much of anything, to be honest. The world won't miss you. They won't be graves with tombstones to visit, they won't be ashes to spread in a lovely location for family to think about every time they want to be close to you. There will be absolutely nothing and no one to care. "

That would be a lie. I had a family now. We weren't conventional, but we were a family, and they would miss me. They would protect me. They would cherish me. All things I spent my whole life without and hadn't even realized how much I craved it until now. I craved being wanted. Belonging. Being loved. And sure, more often than not, I fucking hated Warren. He was an asshole, a prick, a fucking condescending douchebag, but he made no secret ever of his feelings he had toward me even as I fought how I felt about him.

I didn't let on that his words had affected me. "Isn't that the life of the mutant?"

"Could be. I wouldn't know. I have people at home that care about me." He smirked, and I wanted to push him in his crooked fucking teeth, but I stayed calm.

"I bet they will miss you, then."

"I'm not going anywhere," he stated confidently.

"We'll see about that." I wanted to be the one to snuff the life from his eyes. I wanted to watch it drain. I wanted to see him die at my feet as he begged for forgiveness and help from a god that we both knew abandoned us all long ago.

He sneered in my direction before spitting at my feet. "We are moving you in soon. It's a shame that I wouldn't be here to see the face of your beloved beast when he realized he tracked you here into nothing, into a trap for us to capture him."

"You won't succeed." It was a simple fact. I believed in Warren. I trusted him. I knew his judgment. If he got captured by these men, he would surely find a way out. He would make a plan, devise a way out of this situation. I had that much faith in him. I knew him being captured was not a threat.

"Where are you taking her?" Rex's eyes were rimmed with a red I'd not seen before; his fury seeping through.

"Don't worry, freak. You're going with her." He used a sharp metal stick and poked it into Rex's leg, causing him to hiss with pain, but he couldn't pull away, at least not without the chains tightening around his neck. A single move of his wrists would even tighten the chains. He couldn't risk pulling his whole body. "We need leverage to force her to behave."

Rex's eyes tightened shut for a moment as he worked through the pain before he spoke again. "It's cute that you think anyone could force Thea to behave."

"She will. We cannot shed her blood, at least here. We'd prefer the mutant not to go feral until we had him drugged up and captured. But your blood, meh. It's fair game." He poked Rex one more time, and I felt the fury seconds away from boiling over. Could I choke him with my shadows? Would that work? Warren had urged me to show confidence in my ability and push it to its brink, and what better way to push it than trying something new? I pulled the shadows toward me. The darkness slowly crept closer to us when he spoke again. "We'll be back for you. I hope you like car rides."

I released my shadows, letting them snap back into place. Later. Soon. I'd trust myself enough to try the impossible.

I watched until they had backed out of the door and the heavy metal slammed shut, the lock clicking in place.

Then I turned, my eyes set on Rex. "If they are moving us, where will they take us?"

"I don't even know where we are now." He grunted the words out, his jaw clenched as his body remained tight with tension.

He had a point. "I don't understand why they are bothering."

"There are a lot of things I don't understand. But they must have a reason. Maybe to discombobulate our alpha. Not finding you here, but having your scent all over will confuse him." He tilted his head to the side, then cringed as a wave of pain from the chains dug into his body. "They want to use that confusion against him."

"How do you think they will do that?" I leaned my head against his shoulder as we sat.

"I haven't figured out the details."

"Does it hurt?" I asked. "I know it hurts. I can see the red welts and angry skin, but I mean, does it hurt a lot?"

Shit. He clearly was in pain. Why was I even asking? Maybe because I hated to see him hurt. Hated that he had pain I didn't have control of. "I don't feel like going out clubbing at the moment, if that's what you're asking, but it's bearable."

I closed my eyes for a moment and took a deep breath before opening them again. I reached out, pulling my shadows toward us. They danced happily along the floor, glad to be of use once more. When they reached me, I guided them toward Rex, laying them gently against his skin. A hiss left his lips, and he swallowed hard. His eyes nearly rolled back from the relief that the cool touch offered his skin. His lids fluttered. "Fuck, you're perfect."

"Hardly." I laughed as I ran shadowy fingers up and down his skin. It was odd, really. It was almost like the more I pushed my ability with the shadows, the more I used them for things other than hiding myself, the more I could feel through them, the more I could control them, the more they were just an extension of myself. It was almost like I could feel him under my very own fingertips, a whisper of a touch against his skin. I guided the shadows lower, not thinking as I grazed them across his cock. I froze at the exact moment that a slight moan left him.

I could feel that. I sure as fuck could feel that, and it was, well, fucking shocking.

I leaned closer to him. "It does not feel like you're in pain."

"The icy fingers counteract that." He smirked.

"You have no self-control."

"I never had." He looked so damn innocent above the neckline of his clothing. But damn it, remove the shirt and everything about this man screamed danger and trouble. The layers of ink and glistening of his scaled body were like a double whammy to my core. He knew it was too, judging by the cheeky grin he wore. "They left us for a while, you know."

They had, and I knew what he wanted. "And?"

"I've got an itch." He raised a brow at me, which only drew my eyes to that cute little mole he wore right by his eye. I dared to glance lower, catching the dimple before it disappeared from his cheek. "Can you scratch it for me? I can't reach."

"Where?" I crossed my arm, not trusting him for a fucking minute.

He looked down. "My stomach."

Sure. I reached out with my shadows, letting them trail down to his stomach. I imagined them forming a claw with sharp nails before dragging down his body. A hiss escaped through his lips at the feel of the faux nails against his skin. His body leaned into them as the chains rattled and his neck strained. I licked my lips. My heart beating faster had nothing to do with the captivity and everything to do with the pulsing in my lower body at the sight of him.

"Lower," he muttered. "You're too high."

I followed his demand, forcing the shadows to drag lower on his skin, feeling every inch of the surface as if it were my very own fingers touching him and not the shadows I manipulated. I rubbed against his lower abdomen, dancing unseen nails against skin that flexed and tightened under my touch. His voice was a near rasp when he spoke. "Lower."

I pulled the shadows back and released them, letting them snap back to where they belonged in the room's corner, dancing next to the light, then I leaned forward, whispering in his ear as I let my hand roam down his body to cup his dick, "Even the shadows cannot touch things that belong to me."

His Adam's apple bobbed. "Is that so? Am I yours, little Doe?"

I leaned in and nipped at his neck right above the chains before whispering in his ear. "Completely."

He swallowed, the movement straining his throat against the chains. "I'd die for you, Doe. I'd die for you and I'd have no regrets."

I rested my head on his shoulder as I climbed my whole body into his lap. I held on to him tight, hugging him since he couldn't move his arms to hug me back. "You might have to."

Speaking that truth was fucking painful. I didn't want any of these men to die. I didn't think I'd survive it. But I don't think I could stop them from at least trying to protect me. I might be the death of these close-knit friends who grew up together, living family-less on the street, and I could do nothing to prevent it from happening.

He tilted his chin. The chains rattled as they pulled, but that didn't stop him from kissing my head, pressing a kiss on my hair before he let his head fall back. Fuck. The situation he was in made me far more furious than the situation I was in myself. He couldn't fucking move without strangling himself. He never even got a chance to fight this before they had loaded his body with darts and forced him to lose unconsciousness. Funny enough, if you asked me a few weeks ago, I would have thought Ansel would be in this position. But a lot had happened in a few weeks and the notions I had changed. I learned their strengths and weaknesses, their abilities... and I've memorized everything they feel.

"I don't think you're weak," I stated.

"I should have been paying attention." His brows furrowed.

I squeezed my arms around his ribs, hoping I didn't injure him further. I had fully crawled into his lap now, using his body as comfort in this dank cell. "Neither of us were."

"I should have protected you." His words were angry.

"It clearly was my turn to do the protecting." I bit into his shoulder. "I guess I failed too."

"Never." He made a strangled sound when he moved. "You'd never let me down. Even if I was taking my dying breath."

I hated these boys when they talked like that. I hated them for being so realistic of the possibility. It was infuriating to know that they knew well that death was coming to them at some point, and they were so willing to accept it. So willing to lay down their lives for whatever cause they deemed important, but what was more important than me having them in front of me, breathing and alive?

"Don't say that." I scowled at him.

"Say what?"

"About dying. No one is going to die here," I said the words forcefully, like saying them would make them true. But I think we all knew differently. We were aware of the possibility that none of us truly would make it out alive.

"You could silence me." The fucking dimple appeared again, and damn it, didn't he know it made me weak?

"I could." I bit my lower lip as I debated. We were locked in the room, no doubt with eyes on us. It would put me in a vulnerable position, but fuck, wasn't I already vulnerable enough? What difference did it make?

His eyes grew soft before he stuck out his bottom lip. "I'm going to die a virgin, Doe."

I leaned forward and bit into the hard muscle of his shoulder before smacking it. "You're far from a fucking virgin."

"The time gone without sex makes it feel as such," he pointed out.

"It's been like what? Two days."

"A lifetime." His tongue darted out, the long length swiping across my nose as mischievousness danced in his eyes. "A fucking lifetime, Doe."

I rolled my eyes. "Boys are so dramatic. People will watch."

"Let them. Fuck them," he growled, the sound vibrating through my chest. "Fuck them all."

"I could," I teased.

"I'd break these chains before that ever happened," he promised.

"Yeah?" I tried to hide a smirk as I tapped my fingers down his chest.

"It's a promise, Thea."

His eyes burned into me. They were so damn intense it was impossible not to take him seriously. I let my hands fall to his waist again, my fingers brushing against the material. I could feel him against my body, feel his hard length throbbing with want and need. He truly didn't care where we were. He craved the intimacy of us together. I suspected it had nothing to do with the outside world and everything to do with his need to make sure I was fine. Truly, completely fine.

I didn't hesitate to sneak my hands past his waist because he was right. Fuck them. If we were already fleeing death, what harm would it be to steal one last chance at ecstasy? His body tensed. He dared not move, and when my fingers touched the bare skin of his cock; he bit his lip as a rush of air left him. I let my fingers roam over him, took enjoyment in the feel of his soft skin that encased steel. He was so damn perfect. Perfect length. Perfect girth. The most perfect and sweetest of men. How did I get so lucky to land him as my own when I spent my days taking life and hoarding darkness?

"Ride me, Thea," he demanded. "It could be the last time."

"Fuck you," I muttered as I leaned in and captured his lips for a quick kiss. "There will be many times."

"None while I'm in chains locked in a makeshift dungeon." His eyes danced with amusement, but there was nothing amusing about it to me. I didn't want to think of anything happening to him. I didn't want to pretend that this was a fun roleplay. I wanted him to know I fucking cared, and not because of the situation. I cared because I was fondly attached to this group of assholes, somehow. *The mystery was still unsolved for me.*

I reached up, grabbing the chain and pulling hard, forcing his body to tense up as he gasped for air. I released it, and he coughed. "Going to stop making jokes now?"

Another cough. "Probably not."

I didn't think so. Still, I worked the button of his pants before shimmying the zipper down. When cool air hit his cock, a hiss escaped him. His breathing picked up as the anticipation increased, and I couldn't help but wonder how much of that had to do with him and me, and how much of that was knowing they were watching. He liked to watch, but something told me he also liked to be watched.

I leaned down over him, letting my hair curtain around him as my tongue darted out to taste his tip. His hips thrashed upward, the chains rattling as he pulled. He could hardly breathe; wanting only my tongue gliding against his skin. If he were free, I had no doubt that his fingers would already be in my hair, pulling and pushing, demanding what he wanted from me, because in the bedroom was the only time Rex ever demanded. He may take orders from Warren and Ansel without a single complaint, but when it was just the two of us was, he truly held power.

I opened my mouth, taking his whole dick in and loving how fucking wild the single act made him. His hips flexed toward me so damn hard, pushing him as far as he could go, nearly causing me to gag. I pulled upward, dragging my tongue along the underside of his cock until I reached the tip where I swirled my tongue around, teasing him.

We were playing a dangerous game; a game that involved dangerous risks. He was in chains, and though I was free, we were both locked in this cement hellhole waiting for fates to come and collect their dues. Was it stealing to take something so clearly guarded? If so, he was clearly a thief. All of them were because they had no right for stealing the fucks I didn't want to give right out from under me and replacing those fucks with fucking feelings. I didn't want to catch feelings for these men. Hell, I tried to fight it as hard as I fucking could, but now?

"Take it all," Rex demanded.

Now, I'd gladly take it all.

I lowered my lips down his shaft again, taking his full length into my mouth again. My eyes watered, tears streamed down my face, but I couldn't bring myself to care. Not when the sounds I loved hearing so much dropped so flawlessly from his lips, and his hips twitched uncontrollably, even as he fought hard not to move. Rex was controlled and a softy. But I knew for a fact that at this moment, he loved living on the edge. He loved the fight between breathing air and feeling pleasure. He loved to see just how far he could push himself without completely losing control. It was a tightrope. A fine line between blacking out and staying lucid. He strived on toeing the line.

Curses fell from his lips. Demands. Praises. Requests. Each one making my body clench with pleasure. Each one making the pride bubble inside of me. Fuck, how did I live without these men? How had I functioned? I had thought I was happy enough, but it was nothing compared to how I felt when I had Rex under me, taking whatever I gave him with admiration falling from his perfect mouth.

His movements had gotten frenzied, and I knew he was struggling. The chains pulled more, the security of metal wrapped around his throat periodically tightening and loosening as he fought against them to try to claim what he wanted. "Ride. Me. Thea. Please do it."

I looked over my shoulder at the door behind us. It was locked. The hall was dark. If they were coming for us, surely that beep would give them away. And cameras? I was sure they were watching. Probably enjoying the view as they touched their own cocks. The only touch their vile selves would ever fucking receive, for sure.

I sat up straighter before bringing myself to my knees,

hovering my body above Rex's. I only hesitated a single second before I shimmied my pants down my thighs and aligned my core with Rex's cock. Not taking my eyes away from him, I took a deep breath, then lowered myself down, impaling myself onto his cock.

Chapter 7

REX

I COULDN'T HANDLE IT. I was weak. I didn't care who the fuck was watching us. All that mattered was Thea's body around my own. Her tongue was my weakness. The feel of it gliding over my sensitive skin, my downfall. I wanted it all. More of it. Anything she will give. Was I self-ish? Probably. But I didn't care. Thea was mine, after all. Even if she spent so much damn time denying the truth of it, I knew deep down, she knew she would never be free of us. She could never rid of our presence no matter how hard she tried and how much she fought.

I watched through hooded eyes, my chest heaving as my cock disappeared between her lips again. Her hair curtained around her, hiding the indecency from the eyes we knew were prying. I couldn't stand it. My body strained and begged for more from her, begged to feel her body clench against my cock and milk the pleasure from my body. The chains? They pulled and choked, dug into my skin, leaving bruises and scars that I was sure would remain long after the weight of metal was away from my skin.

"Ride. Me. Thea. Please do it," I pleaded again.

I needed it. I craved it. I might die without being inside her tight little body.

She looked over her shoulder toward the door and I knew what she was thinking. I knew the contemplation of being caught, the insecurity of being watched, but none of that mattered when I was around her. Let them watch. Let them loathe that these two freaks of nature had something so fucking unique between them they couldn't even touch the likes of it in their dreams. Fuck them and their superiority. It wouldn't stop me from being close to my female.

Thea turned back toward me, her eyes locked with mine and it was then I saw it—the complete resolve. She had decided and there was no going back. Not that I wanted to. I never wanted to return to any form of life without her in it. If all the change, good and bad, led to this point, I'd never look back. Bring on anything that is after us, because combined, they never would stop us.

Her eyes never left me as she slid her pants down her body, not even bothering to take them off before she took my cock in her hand and positioned herself over my body. I held my breath, afraid to breathe because if I somehow ruined this moment, if I somehow prevented her from following through and her body stealing all the pleasure it needed while using my own, I'd never forgive myself.

The second her body touched mine, I swear I saw stars. My vision blurred as she took my cock into her body, the pleasure so fucking euphoric that for a moment I forgot who I was and where I was, my mind only concentrating on how fucking good she felt, how fucking tight she was, how damn perfect. She held my gaze as she seated herself fully upon me, and the surrounding air burned.

Fire ignited.

Her body wavered with a layer of flames, yet not a single flame burned against my skin.

Orange fire. Turquoise eyes. She was a goddess, and I was not worthy of her body, yet she didn't seem to care. The surrounding fire died down, though I knew what had caused it. She was Warren's. Ours. She no longer could deny that fact. Her eyes didn't leave mine as she rose on her knees before slamming herself back down again. I hissed; the sound left my body involuntarily.

I wished I could touch her.

I fucking wanted to feel her skin against my own. I wanted to hold her hips as I flexed mine into hers and watched her eyes water as she fought to not cum until I demanded her to do so. I wanted to feel the heat of her skin under my fingertips and not just around my cock. I pulled my arms, the movement instantly pulling the chains around my neck, forcing my head to hit the wall as I fought to take in air. Fuck. I just… I just wanted to touch her. I felt like I might die if I didn't.

"Faster," I demanded, and she didn't disappoint. Her body moved up again and back down. Her speed paced with the slight tip of my hips as she dragged my cock inside and out of her body. The feeling of her body encasing my cock was fucking heaven. She was a gift. Our gift. And never in my life had I found something better. "Harder, Doe. Fucking take it all."

I was begging, and it was fucking pitiful, but there was nothing I fucking enjoyed more than having this girl, my mate, stealing and draining all my energy as she captured her own pleasure. It was a work of art, a masterpiece. The way her face morphed and her breathing picked up as pleasure tore through her… Her body fell forward, her nails dug into my chest as she worked toward her peak.

The bite of pain from her nails was euphoric. It reminded me that there was more to this life than remaining in hiding. Why hide when your light and fire blazed as bright as the sun? She could be the sun. She was the light that guided us all.

Fuck. The way she ground herself against me was making me dizzy. I pulled forward, forgetting the chains as they yanked me back. She leaned forward, placing her hands on top of mine before threading our fingers. Her lips were a whisper away from my own when she spoke. "It fucking kills you that you can't be in control, doesn't it?"

"I don't have control issues." I tried to lean toward her lips, but steel dug deep into my flesh.

"If that were true, you wouldn't be nearly choking yourself out right now." She smirked, and the smug face she wore was quickly replaced as she gasped with a single hip movement. "You don't play fair."

"Not when it comes to you." I squeezed her hands. "You aren't fucking me hard enough if you aren't breathless, Doe."

"Is that what you want?" She leaned forward just enough for me to nip at her lips.

"What I want is to be pounding inside of you so hard you don't even know where your body ends and mine begins. I want to have my fingers on your skin so tightly that the creamy white flesh is bruised from my touch. I want to paint your body with my cum and watch you wear it around, stuck to your skin, scenting it like perfume." I swallowed. "But none of those things are feasible right now, are they, Doe? So leaving you breathless, with your skin flush with pleasure and my name a whisper from your lips, is what I'm going to have to settle for."

She captured my lips, giving me a slow kiss as I pulsed with anticipation inside her body. Fuck. I didn't know how she did it. I didn't understand how this one female, this single omega, could bring us all to our knees when never before it had been done. But I'd fall to my knees a million times over if it meant her lips would never leave my skin. It was witchery. A trick of the mind. She had to have the power to get inside our heads because she had every single one of us wrapped around her pinky without even trying.

Thea parted, and I wanted to chase her kiss, if it wasn't for the damn restraints. "Well, I'll guess you'll have to settle for your skin with my bruises, then."

My mouth was so fucking dry. "Settle? Hardly. Give me everything you've got, Doe. All of it."

With a mischievous grin that was borderline sadistic, she gave me every fucking thing she had. She rode me harder, rougher, louder, not fucking caring that every damn person could hear her within a twenty-mile radius. Her skin flamed with heat, fire danced along flesh, her eyes were wild, and every place she ran her finger and dragged her nails would surely leave a bruise.

It was the hottest thing I'd ever seen in my life.

And when she came? I saw fireworks and I don't just mean from the sparks that jumped from her skin and disappeared into the cement. My vision flared to life, flooding with colors and sparks as her pussy squeezed my cock. And when my name fell from those perfect little lips, I lost control. I didn't care about the chains that bound me, not when she said my name at the height of her pleasure. My name. Only mine. I bucked wildly underneath her, pulling and pushing, trying to have more contact with her skin.

Through the gasps for air and the tightening of her body as it tried to milk my cock, she leaned down, her teeth latching on to my skin as she bit. The sharp bite of pain screamed of ownership and loss of control, and it was so fucking hot that I exploded. I couldn't control my hips as they pumped into her, releasing cum in spurts deep inside of her body. Her body squeezed me tighter, draining me of all my pleasure as our chests heaved in unison.

When our orgasms ebbed, and our chests stopped heaving, she rose her head from where it had fallen against the skin of my chest, a wicked grin in place. "Hands down, the best ride I've had in a while."

My chest rumbled with a silent laugh. "I'll make arrangements."

In the distance, the beep rang through the air and Thea stumbled off my body. She pulled up her pants that had settled at her knees, stretched across my body as she had bounced upon me. Then she leaned over and buttoned my pants. "Whatever happens, Rex, we'll get through this."

Get through this? I knew. But how we would come out on the other side? I was terrified. "Of course, little Doe. Nothing can stop us."

The lock turning had both our heads shooting in that direction. Anticipation so fucking thick was in the air that a sharp knife couldn't even slice through it. The door pushed open fully and instead of a few guards, a whole damn team stood in the hall. My heart beat faster. The worry thrummed through me was so intense my stomach churned. But before I had a moment to react, darts rained into the room, hitting their targets before we even realized what was happening.

Thea's hand reached for me, her eyes blinking a few times as the sedative seeped into her system. She tried to struggle, tried to pull me free of the chains, but we both knew it was pointless. We couldn't escape. There was one way out of this room and that exit was surrounded by guards with guns. My head spun as my control slipped. My words sounded far as they left my lips.

"We'll be okay, Doe. I p-promise you this. Warr-en w-would kill t-them all."

Her eyes burned as she looked at me, her face inches away as she still thought to fight the chains to free me. Her hands grabbed tightly to me, her arms finally going limp around my neck as she lost the battle. Her head fell to my shoulders as heavy steps moved forward toward us. Each thump of the step became foggier in my mind. Right before I passed out completely, seconds before the drugs took complete control of my body, a boot stopped in my line of vision.

"She's going to be fucking furious when she learns we darted her for a second time," a voice stated. "I can't fucking wait."

Then the darkness crept into my vision, forcing everything to go black.

Chapter 8

ANSEL

PROJECT GREEK ISLAND.

It was a long-forgotten program that had crumbled long before the collapse of the government. In Greenbrier West Virginia, the program was a presidential bunker under the former Greenbrier Hotel. Before the mutations were even a glint in any doctor's mind, back when foreign affairs were the greatest threat and not the people you grew up next to, the resort was modified as a secret emergency relocation for the former United States Government.

It was a place I would have never thought to examine if it wasn't for the codes that Rodrick had been working on breaking. The hotel hadn't been in operation since the government reformed and now it made sense as to why. It was operating as a secret facility and I was positive that the facility held Thea and Rex.

"For a facility that isn't up and running, it sure is a busy location," I observed from our place afar. I could hear every single sound that echoed from the location, every footfall, every movement. The place was busy. Packed. A bustle of activity for a hotel that was no longer in service and should, by all logic, be abandoned and in disrepair.

"I can smell her. Smell them," Warren growled.

He was barely hanging on. Barely keeping his humanity, knowing that his mate could be in that facility. Having a mate had changed him. He'd always been ruthless, focused, cruel, only when he needed to be. But finding our omega, it focused all those qualities on one being. He'd do anything for her. He'd die for her without hesitation, and though I, too, would do anything for my mate, I feared he would do whatever it takes without thinking of the repercussions.

"The other omega isn't here," I pointed out.

"The other omega isn't my priority at this moment." Warren's words were hard, cold, giving me a clear sign of just how close he was to losing his shit.

"Nor is she mine. However, you need to consider the ramifications of her mere existence. She's important to our cause. All omegas are. If she isn't here, just how many locations of hiding do they have? Anywhere. This land is so damn vast that there could be our omegas hidden away, and we'd never find them. Think about that when you decide to go on a rampage. Our mate is important, but so is knowledge."

"I'd never pick knowledge of others over the safety of our mate." He seethed.

"I never asked that. I'm asking for you to be aware and absorb what information you can when the opportunity presents itself." I sighed. "And to remember that our mate, well, she's as fierce as they fucking come, and I wouldn't doubt that if she found an opportunity, she'd tear down the entire building."

"She is strong." I heard the slight static of our devices before he continued. "Rodrick's team is almost to the capital. They'll be waiting and ready from there. Our job is to get her and Rex and meet them there. Do you think we can handle that?"

"Have you forgotten who you are talking to?" I teased, though there was no joy behind it. I was a savage with a knife, and I hoped he knew that I always had his back. I was a somebody he could always count on, even if the morals of the situation were murky.

"Do you have your weapons?"

I almost rolled my eyes. I was more armed than he was. But then again, he had the advantage of sight, a gift I hadn't had since I was a child. "I've got them everywhere. You name it, and I'm sure it's sharp."

"Borrowing Rex's belt buckle, then." I felt the humor in his words. The stupid, hideous buckle was in a shape of a razor blade, and damn it, it was smart because it actually hid sharp objects inside in addition to the edges.

"He's going to be furious," I confirmed.

"All the commotion is around the back of the building. We enter from front."

"Fly in?" I questioned.

"It's getting dark. They wouldn't see that approach. And it's faster." And fast mattered when you were trying to get into a facility and rescue your mate.

"You just want to snuggle. Admit it," I teased as I stood, brushing off the dirt and dried grass that had stuck to the leg of my slacks.

"Not unless you've got raven hair and crystal eyes." He snorted. "Let's go. No one is out front."

No one? Which was cause for concern. Why would

they leave the entire front of the building unguarded? "It's a setup."

"We walk in anyway," he stated. "I can smell her from here, and I will not risk her discomfort any longer."

I could smell her, too. She was here or had been. "It could be a trap to capture you."

"Let them." He stood; the sound of his clothing rustling. "I'd rather her be safe."

"But the capital. We have a bigger picture, Warren, and Thea would understand that," I tried to reason with him, but he would have none of it.

"There is no bigger picture without Thea. She was meant to take control, to lead. To appeal to both humans and mutants. A female leader is unheard of, you know this. Never in the history of this land had we had one. She would be backed by mutants, females, humans, mothers, families... She has a greater chance of succeeding." He cracked his knuckles, the sound making me cringe. "None of that will happen if we don't save her first. She's family and she's—"

He let his words hang. He was worried. I understood. If our plan went as we had hoped, as we had worked out for years before finding her, Thea wouldn't just be our mate, she would grow our family. A fact he was positive that he had already accomplished while she was in heat. Which makes him unable to think as clearly as he should. Thea may be the perfect person to take power, but without him at her back, that power wouldn't last. We needed them both safe. Both unharmed.

"We'll get her," I confirmed because there was no other option. I stepped forward, slung the alpha over my shoulder, fighting not to make a joke about how much of a damsel he was at this moment. Then I flew, following the sound, clicking my tongue to locate the building. With Warren's help, I dropped us down in a cluster of decorative trees, our presence unseen.

I followed him as he led the way closer to the building and wished we had insisted on more backup. Him and me? We were capable. But we didn't know what we were walking into, and wasn't Rex and Thea equally capable before they were sedated from a distance and brought to unconsciousness?

We walked in the front door, a fact that was making my stomach tighten. If the door wasn't guarded, did they expect us? They had to have. Unless they thought we weren't smart enough to locate them, thus not needing protection. But they had to know that an alpha could follow their omega anywhere. All it took was time and tracking, right? Had they studied other alpha and omega pairings? Did they know this?

"The door shouldn't have been unguarded," I mentioned, whispering so that no one could hear us as we stepped across the tile flooring. The whole first floor was abandoned. Everyone appeared to be in the backyard area, fussing with a few vans that Warren had mentioned were parked. "This doesn't sit well."

He ignored my concern, but I knew he knew I was right. "There should be an entrance to the bunker below through a ballroom's false wall."

"It could be a trap," I continued.

"It probably is." he responded as we moved forward. I clicked my tongue softly, listening. "I think the ballroom entrance is here."

The clinking of metal was soft as he pushed down the knob and opened the door with a shove. With a click of my tongue, I didn't have to guess to know what type of space we were in. A large open room, unobstructed. Every warning bell imaginable went off in my head, telling me we should turn back, regroup, wait until we have someone with us, more people at our backs. But there was no turning back now, no leaving this place unseen.

I followed the sound of Warren's footsteps as he walked toward the wall. When he stopped, the sound of his palm rubbing against the wallpaper told me he was already searching. "It's one of these panels, along one of these walls. I just… I don't know how to open it. Rodrick didn't know that part."

I stood back for a moment, not sure where to start, before I stepped forward, running my hands against the panels. I pushed, felt around for buttons, knobs, anything that would show that this was the place that held some sort of secret opening behind it. Nothing. I had moved five panels in the opposite direction of Warren and was just about to continue further along when I felt it.

A draft.

A slight breeze that tickled against my skin. It wasn't from above, or from the flooring where vents usually were located, it seemed to be coming from the seams of the wall, between panels. I placed my hand in front of it, pausing for a moment to take in the feel of air against my skin before I announced, "Here. There's a breeze between this panel and the next."

Warren was at my side in seconds. His hands roamed the wall with mine. "I'm not finding the mechanism."

"It's here." I knew it was. The breeze still tickled the fine hairs on my forearm, taunting me with what it was hiding behind this wall. Giving me hope that if we just got this open, we'd be inside, closer to getting our mates and getting the hell out of this place. The unease tripled with each step we took, and the sooner we got in and left this property, the sooner we could be on our way to the capital, knee-deep in infiltration plans that the good ol' president of the United Government never saw coming. There was nothing fucking united about being under his rule. Not one damn thing.

In a room over, a door shut, and footsteps thumped against the polished wood floor. "Someone is coming."

Warren cursed. His movements became frantic as he searched around. I dropped to my knees, my hands pushing and feeling for any sort of indication that this wall would give way to an opening. The breeze this low intensi-fied, seeming to seep from below and from the sides. It was here; I knew it. I was positive about it.

The footfall increased, the sound of voices just outside the main door to the ballroom growing louder as they approached.

We were out of time. It was now or never, because if they found us here, we would have no choice but to kill. Kill or be killed. When you were a mutant, those were the only options, and as much as it went against normal morals, I'd kill every single time.

The door to the ballroom's handle jiggled, and my stomach sank. I whispered to Warren, "They're here."

"I know." He sounded defeated, though I knew that nothing ever really defeated the man. I was just about to stand up, ready to fight, when my finger felt an indent in the wallpaper. It was slight, and I was positive that if anyone with normal senses were to touch the spot, they might not have noticed. But I wasn't exactly normal. I felt things, smelled things, heard things that nobody else could, and because of that, the slight circular indent caught my attention.

"I think I've—" I didn't hesitate to press it, and with the pressure of my fingers on the circle, the door popped open.

Warren was pulling it wide enough for us to fit through before I was fully in a standing position. The door on the other side of the room opened, and I shoved Warren into the opening, forcing him in before me. I slid inside, pulling the door closed behind me right as footsteps stepped into the room.

Chapter 9

WARREN

MY PALMS WERE SWEATING as we searched for the entrance to the bunker It was quite difficult, considering all the walls looked the same. There weren't any signs that we would find the entrance here. Hell, a lot had changed in the years since this place had been in commission. A lot had changed in this world, too. We had changed; we had changed this world and though I'd like to think our existence had morphed and formed it for the better; I wasn't naïve enough to think that there weren't people out there who disagreed.

My fingers ran over the wallpaper that was so extremely outdated it should be a war crime, as I searched for any signs that the entrance could be behind the panels. We needed in; it was our only hope. Thea's scent was so damn strong now that my dragon roared with displeasure, painfully clawing at my skin. He wanted his mate, but fuck, he wasn't the only one. I felt like I was abandoned in a desert without a drop of water when she was not around. Slowly deteriorating, my will to exist dissipating.

Dramatic? Maybe.

But my flare for drama didn't cancel out the fact that I may never sleep again unless her knife is securely pointed at my heart. I wanted all the things I had experience for such a short time. I wanted the feisty brunette in my bed and on my cock. I wanted the knife fights and struggle for power. I wanted my fucking omega and I would do anything to get her back.

The humans were getting closer and, though I wouldn't give up my search until the very last moment; I was panicking inside. Because if we had to start off in a rage of murder and blood, there was no way we'd make it to Thea before things went to shit. We needed to remain stealthy for as long as possible; a task that we couldn't do when there were people approaching.

The steps grew louder as they neared us, and when they stopped in front of the ballroom door, I didn't need Ansel's announcement to let me know they had approached. I felt the weight of defeat, knowing that in seconds, a minute, if lucky, we'd have to break into chaos when all I wanted to do was find my calm. "I know."

The weight of despair was heavy, and my body drooped against the useless fucking panel, my forehead resting against the monstrosity of wallpaper for a moment. "I think I've—"

Ansel never had a chance to fully push the mechanism and get off his knees before I was in his space, practically prying the door open and pushing my body through it. I didn't give a fuck that it was black as night on the other side and I hadn't a clue where I was going. I only cared about not getting caught and buying ourselves a few extra minutes of time. He pushed his body through, and the door slammed, whooshing air toward us as it sealed shut.

Holding our breath was near impossible, with our hearts racing so damn fast. Still, we managed as we listened for the steps to grow closer, hoping we hadn't been spotted shutting the door. Nobody came, and when we finally could relax, we wasted no time moving around the space. I pushed my arm out, searching for walls, not shocked when my fingers touched a steel stair railing.

"I could never be you," I muttered to my partner.

"No one could," he replied instantly. "It's impossible to be this badass."

Cocky. He was in my unit, so I'm not even shocked at that fact. "I've found a stairwell. Do you need help?"

"Do you?" he countered.

Touché.

I took the steps down quietly, knowing I shouldn't rush, but damn it, I fucking wanted to. I wanted to rush into the space, enemy be damned, and find my woman. I reached the bottom of the stairwell and a faded light blinked on and off, barely holding on as it threatened to die. There was a door, a massive thick metal door, one that would withstand fucking anything at nearly two feet thick. It was built to last.

And it had lasted.

It lasted through the fall of the government and into the creation of another. If I played my cards right, it would last through the downfall of that one and the creation of something greater. Stronger. More inclusive and logical than those before it.

Ansel followed me as we stepped into the open door. "There are hallways. All empty."

"My gut is telling me to abort."

"And mine is telling me he will slash me open from the inside if I don't keep going," I responded.

But he was right. Something felt off. Unnatural. And despite that, I refused to turn back. I refused to care about my well-being when my mate was missing, and her scent coated every surface of this building. I stepped lightly against the tile, ignoring the glow of the fluorescent light that was way too bright for this space. Doors were wide open, but none of them called to me until I reached toward the end. I stopped, freezing for a moment before moving forward.

Rex. Rex has been here, and if I had to guess, it wasn't pleasant for him. I pulled back from the room, moving a little further, ignoring the entrances to halls and offices. Not caring that they had meeting rooms and bunks down here. She hadn't been in any of them. But the room at the very end? I inhaled, closing my eyes for a second longer than normal to take in the scent of her.

She was there. I could smell the faint trails of her blood and taste molecules of fear. But I knew my girl enough to know she would fight it, pretend that there was not a single thread of fear within her, and fight. I pushed through the door of the room, finding it empty of people, but the medical equipment remained. Syringes, needles, scalpels were placed orderly on trays, and in the middle of the room, a table with straps, and chains lying on the floor nearby.

They had restrained my mate? The thought made me physically ill. A low rumble began in my chest and forced its way upward. Ansel reached out, his hand on my shoulder. "She is stronger than what sights plague you."

I hope so. I fucking did. But every part of me wanted

to blanket her in my protection and ensure that not a single finger of human scum touched her again. It was a promise I made myself, a swear to protect the most precious of gifts this world had bestowed upon me. I moved forward through the room, picking up pieces of equipment, smelling tools and picking up scents. Every one of them, every scent of the humans that had touched my mate with malice in their hearts, will die. There was no other choice in the matter.

With a drop of a metal clamp onto a metallic tray, I turned and left the room. I breathed deep, soaking up the scents, filtering, finding my mate. The coils of her scent led me to a door and behind it a new set of stairs. Without hesitation, my feet hit the steps, Ansel's behind me as I plowed down. At the bottom, there were some drips of blood. New, but dried. I inhaled at the same time as Ansel.

"Not our mate," I announced.

The corner of his lip tilted up. "Not our mate. But I'm sure our princess had no problem being the one inflecting the pain."

Princess. Never would I have thought of her as such, but now? Didn't we hold her on a pedestal and treat her with such favor that we make no secret of who is superior? "She wouldn't have hesitated."

The trail of blood drops went on a few feet where they stopped, assuming stunted by something to aid in the flow. We continued walking through the narrow hallway until we got to another door. On the outside, a large lock sat with a keypad. But the door was propped open, leaving it vulnerable to intruders like me. I wondered, how many intruders did they get here? None? Some? Were we the first?

"The doors propped open," I informed Ansel.

"I'm warning you, it's a trap." His brows pulled together. "We can turn back."

"And leave the rest of our team possibly in danger?" I grabbed hold of the door. "I'd never. You know me better than that."

"They aren't there," he pleaded. "You're walking into a trap knowingly, Warren."

"And you likely will follow." I stepped into the room. "If she isn't here, she is somewhere and I will find out either way."

"We have no way of informing Rodrick. Our equipment doesn't work down here." Ansel was always level-headed, always the voice of reason, and I didn't need a reason right now. I needed my mate, alive, in front of me. I needed to feel her skin against my own. Feel her raw need for my body as she pulsed and squeezed around my cock. I didn't care that if I went in, I wouldn't be going out. I only cared that going in meant I could be closer to her and places she had been since she left us. If she had been down this hall, I needed to find out why.

Without waiting for further refusal, I walked in and released the door. He could follow, or he could not. It did not matter to me that his self-preservation was more prominent in his mind than the state of our mate. Our priorities may be different, but the endgame would be the same. I was planning to plow through, take on whatever attack they wanted to give me, knowing damn well they would reunite us. He wanted to backtrack, plan, approach from another angle. Both meant going after our mate, but only one meant getting there faster.

He followed, and I could feel the anxiety smothering him as we walked. We took the hall slowly. The surroundings were nondescript. When we reached another open door, I knew. I knew for a fact that on the other side, my mate had been. I could smell her. I could smell Rex. I could smell the lust and pleasure that had been released from them both, nearly taste it in the air around me, and it comforted me to know that they were together here and not separated for the extent of being down here in this concrete hell.

I entered the room with Ansel close behind. The scent of Rex's blood was heavy here. The metallic smell coated the surfaces and hadn't yet been washed away. What had they done to him? They'd pay for hurting him, too. I walked through the center of the room and to the chains that were threaded on the wall. I picked them up, the metal cold against my fingers, but the flakes of blood that were stuck to them were still warm. It was Rex's. The blood of my family laced these chains, and it didn't matter how many deep breaths I took, because each one only fueled the fury that was growing inside of me.

"These chains held Rex," I growled the words out to Ansel, knowing damn well he couldn't see what I saw, but he could feel what I did. "There is blood on them."

"There is blood, but the scent of lust is strong. He is well enough," Ansel pointed out, though the logic still made him tense. He could try to soothe me and maybe it worked. But Rex was still here and hurt, and Thea was with him.

"Well enough, sure. But they drew blood, and that, well, it doesn't sit right with my dragon. My need to protect what's mine is strong. Thea may be my mate, but Rex is my best friend, my family, my partner in life choices since we were teens, and fuck them if they think they could make him bleed and get away with it."

Ansel stepped forward, his hand out until he touched the cool metal. "I think they sealed whatever fate the minute they drove sedative darts into our family. I have no judgment for whatever their actions force you to do."

He leaned forward, his eyes blinking a few times.

"What is it?"

I questioned him not because I thought he knew something I didn't, but because since Thea entered our lives, things have been changing. Him blinking rapidly was something I was not used to. He never showed that type of reflex. He squinted his eyes shut before he looked back at me, his stare the blank black orbs I was used to. "It's nothing. I just thought..." He tilted his head for a moment before righting it. "For a second, I swear I saw the chains in my hand."

Muscle memory? Could what he was feeling in his fingers and the strength of his brain be filling in the voids? Was that possible? Or was it because since Thea entered our life, everything that was once impossible became so fucking tangible that nothing could truly shock us any longer? "Has it happened before?"

"Not many times," he admitted. "But it has."

"When?" I prompted as I turned around, walking the length of the dinky cell, examining every nook and cranny. There wasn't much. A camera in the corner. Was it on? An unused bucket in the corner, and cement wall barriers that kept the occupants of this cell from the outside world against their will.

"When my cock was buried inside of her." I turned, looking directly at him, though his eyes indicated he couldn't see me doing so. "I saw her eyes. The color. And since then, since that moment, flashes of things I'd not seen since I was child. Brief. Quick. As if my eyes are trying to figure out how they need to work but can't grasp it."

It was Thea. I fucking knew it. "She was meant for us."

In the distance, a buzz sounded, and our heads turned. It was the first sign of life we had experienced down here, and yeah; we expected a shit show to have already rained down upon us, but knowing it was approaching gave a different type of anticipation. Should we run? Should we try to escape? Should we fight back and slaughter every single human that attacked in retribution for what they had done to our family? What we should do was still a blur, but what I wanted to do was wear the blood of my enemy against my skin like a coat of accomplishments and strut in the street.

Did that make me deranged? Maybe. But those plagued with madness had way more fun.

Footsteps.

Rapid footsteps moved toward us and I tried to count them, but there were so many. Twenty. Thirty. More than enough to fit in this room. "We are outnumbered."

"I tried to tell you," Ansel muttered.

"Our game plan?" I smirked, knowing there was only one option.

"Cause some damage. Make a stir. Then when we go down, knowing we took out way more of them." Ansel walked to the wall, next to the doorframe, and I followed, taking position on the opposite side. He slowly rolled up the sleeves of his shirt up to his elbow before taking out a knife. "I hope I don't need to use this hideous buckle."

"I hope you do," I stated, my words drowned out by the sound of the heavy footfalls. "I fucking hope you do."

The first men through the door hadn't a damn chance of survival. Our weapons sliced through their skin like butter, cutting open their flesh and tendons, peeling it away from their bones with one swoop and then another before they stumbled forward, gargling on their own blood. Their hands held their throats, as if that would stop the flow of life that was leaving their body, but it helped nothing. There would be no saving them.

The nearly positive death of their fellow men didn't detour the next people from entering. They pushed through the door, nearly falling and stumbling on each other to make it inside, hoping we didn't slaughter them in the process. It was chaos, but men like Ansel and I fed on chaotic moments, and it only fed our power and strengthened our intentions.

Bodies laid dead at our feet; all sent to their deaths like sacrificial lambs. They didn't know any better. They hadn't woken this morning thinking about their upcoming death, yet the government placed as little value on their lives as they did my own. They were tools to be used, and it was unfortunate. It was so fucking unfortunate because in a situation such as this, I'd pick my life over theirs and I wouldn't feel the regret over the loss and the pain their families must endure.

It was a gap of humanity that was thrust toward us and forced down our throats. We were forced to care for people like us and fuck those who weren't. Until positions were switched, until Thea had control, and the fucking president, the man who started this all, was dead, we couldn't begin to breech the differences between us and heal from the lies that both sides were told.

Blood coated the ground, and none of it was mine. Not a single drop from Ansel. All of it was of the humans', who the government deemed invaluable. All of it signaling a loss of a life. I waited for regret, a single thread of regret to appear somewhere inside of me, but it never came. I was numb to the effects of society, numb to the fact that we had become a disposable nation in the most horrific of ways.

A canister rolled into the room, nestling itself between two lifeless bodies. I looked up toward Ansel, though his gaze was nowhere meeting mine. It was too far out of our reach, too far for me to grab it and toss it back out before it detonated. I didn't have to tell him as much, without even seeing what we were up against. He knew.

"Take a deep breath," he reminded me, and before the last word left his mouth, smoke was already filling the air. The unmanageable feel of pepper tickled my throat, the sting crawled downward, searing into my esophagus before my eyes poured out tears. The inflection didn't stop our defenses; it only made it harder to inflict pain on others, made it harder to see where my blow would land when I could barely open my eyes. It meant that the men were slipping through, getting past us, and if they got past us, it meant we were losing the upper hand.

We knew this moment would come. Ansel warned me about it repeatedly. But that didn't mean we didn't inflict as much damage on those advancing as we could. My arms were growing tired, my body scraped with nicks and bruises from well-placed fists. My clothes were red from blood, and my eyes and throat felt like fire. We were no longer the ones in control, and I was okay with that. With people at my back and still entering through the door, I was aware I was surrounded, but I didn't fear the capture.

The capture meant Thea.

The capture meant I could find my mate and save her from whatever tortures she is enduring.

The capture meant death to all those who thought they could contain and mute the mutants and beasts when all we ever wanted was to be heard.

I held back in this fight. I held back the animal I was. I refused to suck down the delicacy of any soul and let it slide down my throat to fill my body lustfully when I could save that strength for later. I could save my ability for the moments when my body was too physically tired to protect my mate, but my mind was unwilling to give up.

The armored bodies entered; their faces covered by a thick layer of plastic that protected them from the smoke that filled the space. Their weapon was poised as they pointed at us. There was nothing more we could do, no more fight to be had for us, at least not here. "Weapon down, Ansel."

I let him know about the things he couldn't see. He didn't hesitate. His palm opened, and the copper-soaked blade fell to the ground, clinking against the cement floor before finding its resting place. There was a moment of silence in the room, where everyone held their breaths, waiting to see what happened next. It was hard, felt nearly impossible, really. But I forced myself forward, forced myself to open my fists and release the weapon that was practically a part of me. It fell to the floor, not clinking with satisfaction as Ansel's weapons had, but landing on the soft flesh of the dead.

The weapons that were suddenly at my back dug in hard, sending a jolt of pain through my spine. The man in front of me turned, the barrel of his gun pointed at Ansel, and it was in this moment I realized maybe I had miscalculated. What if there wasn't a dart inside of there, as I suspected? What if I was the only man they wanted alive? Had I traded Ansel's life so that I could get what I wanted, when I wanted, as fast as possible? If we had waited, if we had pulled back, if I had allowed us to form a solid plan, then approach, would it have been different?

I hadn't thought this through.

I knew we were walking into danger, and I forced him.

His death would be on my hands. The death of my best friend.

If those weren't darts, that would mean—

A slight click broke the silence before a low rumble and whoosh of air and then it was too late to wonder what if I had done something different. The trigger had been pulled... and Ansel? Right in the path of the weapons' projection.

Chapter 10

THEA

I BLINKED. My eyes dry, my throat on fire. My pulse thrummed through my forehead, pounding. This surely wasn't a fucking good time. More blinking and then my gritty eyes allowed me to open them fully without shying away from the light. My thoughts were heavy, thick, and just to grasp a single one, I had to swim under murky water and fight to reach it.

My gaze roamed around an unfamiliar room, so white that the color hurt my pupils. There was nothing around me, no furniture, no people, and for a moment, I wondered if I had died. I wondered if our lives were no longer useful to them. Had they caught Warren? Did they capture what they wanted, and now they had disregarded our existence and murdered us while we were in an unconscious state? The door beeped.

I closed my eyes, afraid to look. When I opened them again, black leather shoes broke the mundane of the white flooring. I followed the shoes up a body until my eyes landed on a familiar face. "Nice to see you again, Thea."

The feelings were not mutual. In fact, now seeing my former mentor only made my body be consumed by repulsion. I didn't bother to answer him. He could read my thoughts and feelings regarding him through my expression that I didn't try to mask. His eyes roamed over me for a moment more before he tapped a button on the wall. In seconds, a woman in white stormed into a room, handing over a metal box to Jerome Kent.

Her feet carried her swiftly away before he turned back to me, box in hand. "I bet you're wondering what's in this box, aren't you?"

I didn't answer. I let my eyes rest hard on his, not bothering to glance at the box. Yeah, I wondered. But he wanted that reaction. He wanted that wonder. He wanted me to beg him to show me what was in the box. I also knew that whether I wanted to see it or not, it didn't matter. He'd show me. He'd open that box after he got his villainous speech out of the way and reveal whatever important piece of information he'd been hiding.

"Not feeling wordy? No worries." He sat on the edge of my bed, and I tried to pull away from his nearness, but the tingling in my limbs prevented me from moving. My mind had come back fully, but my body hadn't yet caught up. "How's the bed? Comfortable? I hope so. You know, Thea... I never thought this would play out this way. I thought maybe we would use you, keep you under our thumbs until you were old and wise enough to be killed; after doing the work for us, of course. If we had known you would have attracted the attention of the strongest of freaks out there, we'd have planned better."

He wasn't a freak. And fuck Kent for thinking so.

Warren was more of a man, even with his mutation, than the male sitting next to me.

Kent fiddled with the metal box before he pushed the lid open. He looked inside for a moment, a proud smile curving his lips before he reached inside and pulled out a controller. He held up the control in front of me; the buttons gleaming brightly against the black plastic. "What's this, Thea? Come on, I know you're smart enough to know."

I knew what it was, but what it went to, I had no clue. I hadn't even tried to figure that out yet. I licked my dry lips, trying to force words out. "It's a... it's a control. A remote. "

He smiled widely, and never in my life had I hated a man more than him this very second. I had envied him once, cared about him as if he was family. The admiration clearly only went one way, and that knowledge stung. He nodded his head at me as if I was a child, barely able to comprehend basic thoughts. "Good job. It is a remote, and before you ask because I know you're wondering, this remote activates and controls this."

He reached inside of the box he held and pulled out a strip of metal about an inch wide and a few inches in length. On one side, a key hung, and the way Kent's hand bent and formed the metal, I suspected it was meant to form a circle. I blinked a few times, my mind still fuzzy. But, fuzzy or not, I caught on to the implications. A circle with a lock... a control... a ... a fucking collar.

His grin widened as my realization spread. "That's right, my girl. Now, this is an important step. We've collected your mutant. We've got him secured in this same location as you. I wonder... can you feel him here? Can you smell him? He's not been on this floor. No... this floor was reserved for the very miracle that was you."

"I'm not a fucking miracle." I ground my back teeth, hating this man more and more each second and wishing I wasn't strapped down so that I could prove to him.

"Oh, but you are. We've had many omegas in one of our many facilities. But never had we been able to catch an alpha that matched with any of them. We were going to kill you. That was always the plan. Use you as bait and kill you off. But the tests... the tests were so damn interesting. We'd had all the omegas... but never a fertilized one. I wonder, Thea, what will happen when you give birth to a little monster like yourself? We'd never seen it happen. All of our experiments had failed. Nothing seemed compatible. But now? You're giving us the impossible."

Panic rose. My palms grew clammy. The thought of what he had said to be true, unfathomable. I... We couldn't have created life. That was impossible. It was impossible, and it aligned with everything that Warren had claimed and I'd refused to believe. Fuck, if the circumstances were different, that man would gloat for days. But they weren't different. Now I had just fallen into the hands of the enemy and become their most favorite of experiments to date. I wouldn't let him know he scared me. I refused to let on that the words he spoke were just as terrifying as the actions that were sure to follow.

"I'm sure you know by now that this collar here is for you. We'll keep Warren in line by threats to you."

"If you think he would care that I had this collar around my neck, you're wrong," I spat out the words. "Warren only cares about himself."

Complete lie. But he didn't need to know just how deep our attachment went. Kent's brow rose in challenge. "Is that so? I suspect when he learns the joyous news, he will care a fuck lot."

Joyous news? Was it? I didn't know how I felt about it. I

wasn't motherly, and fuck, the world had to know that this, whatever this situation was, was not what I had planned. Not in the least. But despite that, I didn't hate the idea that there was a piece of us that strived together to form what I could only imagine was a better, mini version of ourselves. I bet Rex would be amazing with our child. The corner of my lips quirked involuntarily at the thought before another realization slammed into me.

"Where is Rex?"

"Reginald is with his friends."

"Excuse me?" Reginald? He leaned over me, clicking the collar in place before I even realized it was happening. A turn of the key had the collar locked on.

"Yes. Reginald. Hadn't you known?" I had better get to him before I die just so I could gloat about his name. "Anyway, he's with Warren and Ansel. But don't you worry, Thea, you're the prized possession here now, not the dragon. His value, though still great, decreased after we saw the results of the test we had run on you. The gift you're giving us? Astronomically generous."

Without thinking, I propelled my body forward, pulling all the shadows I could find in this seemingly shadowless room toward me, ready to attack, but my body was met by a jolt of electricity coming from his collar, stopping me in its track. His claim sent fury through me and there was nothing I could do about it. I had no power here, not with the collar around my neck, and he knew it. I never wanted this. I never asked for Warren, or Ansel, or even Rex. I never wanted what came with our relationship. But now? I felt protective over what we had created together, and I would die before it landed in his hands.

"We will kill you," I threatened.

"You can try," he countered before patting my knee at the same time he sent a spark of electrical current into me.

"Now, I've got control of this, and I'll continue to do so when you meet our country's leader for the first time. Don't worry, your monsters will be there too. A reunion of sorts. Get dressed, Thea. I'm taking you to stretch your legs before dinner. You've got to work off some of that sedative." Another pat on the leg. "Don't worry; it was composed of safe compounds so as to not hurt our little lab rat you're harboring."

He stood up, using the remote to flex the powers one last time, making my teeth clash together with the voltages. Sure, the compounds were safe, but this? This can't be, right? He walked toward the door, and when his fingers touched the knob, he froze before turning slowly. "Oh, and, Thea... I'll be waiting outside this door. Dress swiftly and don't be creative... I'm not in the mood for craftiness."

I sat for another minute after he left, trying to force myself to rise slowly to avoid any dizziness from those damn darts. I tried to think for a brief second of a way out of this, but ... there was none. Not until I had this collar off my neck and my men at my side. Until then? I had to comply. I was forced to. If I didn't, I might never see them again, and I needed to have them close to me. When we were together, we were stronger and operated as one. Mentally, physically, emotionally stronger. We needed each other to thrive.

I found some clothes folded in a neat stack at the end of my bed. White, crisp, clean cloth that under normal circumstances I would never wear. But wearing white clothing was far better than the sheet that was tucked around me. How I had lost all my clothes and when it had happened were thoughts I hadn't wanted to think about. What they had done to my body while I was unconscious left a helpless feeling that threatened to turn me hysteric. But hysteric wasn't my way. Revenge was, and one day, hopefully soon, I'd have my revenge on these men.

I dressed up in the pants and shirt quickly, before putting on a pair of hard bottomed slippers onto my feet. The door was unlocked, and when I pulled it open, Kent was waiting in the hallway, his hands behind his back as he leaned against the wall. I had no doubt that if I looked behind him, his fingers would clutch the device meant to cause me harm. He knew me well; he trained me, after all. My capabilities were what he taught me, though I was stronger than just my ability to play with the knives.

"Just so you know, Thea. That little shock I'd gifted you with was merely a demonstration of what that collar around your neck was capable of. Don't be stupid. I don't want to prove further the power you're up against. Follow me."

But did he realize the power he was up against, too? The power and strength Ansel, Rex, Warren, and I had when we were together. The force we put forth to protect those we loved? I would do anything to protect them, and if Kent hadn't realized that yet, he would. He would learn soon enough and then it would be too late for him.

I followed him, tracking each turn of the hallway, each window, door, room. Any knowledge could be helpful, just as it could be useless if not relevant. I'd take my chance, I'd memorize everything. I'd do anything to come out of this alive with my family intact.

It wasn't until we had exited the building and entered a garden that it hit me where we were. "Is this—"

"The White House? Yes." He let out a little laugh. "You know, they were planning to demolish this place after the government fell, but I talked them out of it. This place had stood for leadership and control for so damn long it would be harder for the people to blindly follow us in the new government reform without this dull building backing us up. This landmark has power. It falsely persuades the people into security, and they somehow, for some fucking reason, oddly accept that if you control a simple building, you control it all. It's not true, as you know. But how easy was it to hand over control to us when they thought there was no longer any other option?"

"Why bring me here?" I asked. I wanted information. All the information. Anything I could get from this man that could better prepare me for what I was up against.

"The garden? Well, I thought we would pick some flowers to be used for the centerpieces at tonight's dinner. You're not really the floral type, but that doesn't mean others don't enjoy flowers to brighten the mood."

He picked up a basket, and in it was a pair of shears. I eyed them, wishing I could use them to end his life, but knowing that I'd never get that far. Not with the rows of guards that lined up everywhere. I'd wait. I'd buy time until the world aligned for me and I could end this all. At least, I hoped.

"I meant, why am I at the capital?" I followed behind him as he strolled toward the array of flowers.

"We need to keep you close, Thea. And the men you are attached to? Well, Warren and our leader of the reformed government have a history. They needed time to talk it out."

"Excuse me?"

"Do you know who the people, and by people, I mean us, not the public, picked to rule the United Government?" He proceeded. "What do you think of this rose?"

"It's good. No. No I don't," I admitted. Should I? Probably, though, I doubted the information granted me would be that shocking. Every man in this government had proven to be scum.

"Did you know that under this very building, there is a large government facility for research and science? It had been here since the beginning and not a single person ever questioned it." He pondered as he cut some roses and placed it into the basket. "Why? Because sometimes ignorance really is bliss. It's not as active as it once was; now it's merely for important cases. But back in the day..."

He looked off into space as if he was reliving a glorious memory, and the urge to stab him with the shears grew. I hated the betrayal I felt when I looked at him. Despised him for luring me into false respect and admiration for years, only to learn the heartbreaking truth that his comfort and care were placed on me not at a desire to shelter and care for me as a lost kid of the streets, but to use me as the government had demanded.

Kent suddenly turned to me; his interest piqued. "Well, you'll learn soon enough about the facility under the capital. For now, can you appreciate a good daisy in a bundle of flowers?"

I felt emotionless as I glared at him. "Daisies are perfect."

"Good." He smiled, though it was false. "You're feeling all right now?"

"Like it matters. You drugged me, remember?" I pointed out, though, I was feeling a bit off. My legs still felt heavy from the sedative, and my head throbbed.

His hand waved dismissively, the shears coming close to piercing my skin with the action. "It was to protect you."

"I didn't need protection," I stated.

"Trust me, you are a danger to yourself sometimes, Thea." He reached over and cut off a rose. "We couldn't have you doing something stupid and ruining the chances of life for the newest member of our team."

He, nor anyone he worked with, would ever get any

child of Warren's. He was delusional if he thought so. Warren would tear him to pieces, Ansel would carve his body, and Rex? He'd proudly operate as the clean-up crew.

He continued talking like I wasn't picturing his body in a pile of blood at my feet. "I need you to behave tonight when you meet the president. Emotions will be high, and I understand that, trust me. But he is the ruler of the new free nation and he demands respect."

"Free nation?" I laughed humorlessly. "It's only free if you look like you. If you're like any of us who were unfairly created, freedom is a dream that may never be obtained."

"Trust the process, Thea. It's better that way. Imagine if men like Warren ran around freely. It would be a catastrophe."

I pictured Warren, Ansel, and Rex with Gia and the rest of her family, pictured them with the entire community they created and protected. "It would be a masterpiece."

"You always liked destruction." He reached for a white carnation and paused, waiting for my approval. I nodded, not really giving a fuck about the flowers, but not wanting to fight it. "The meal tonight might get tense, but it's imperative you keep your cool. Those men feed off your energy and if you aren't collected, I don't imagine they will be."

They didn't feed off my energy. I was positive I fed off theirs. I gained an exponential amount of energy from each orgasm they gifted me. I felt more alive than I ever had when I was surrounded by them, secured in knowing I had backup for whatever we faced. "I will not rein them in, if that's what you're asking. They are free from me at the very least in this awful place. I will not control them."

"You could. It's part of what an omega does."

Was that even true? I doubted it. They would willingly do anything I asked. "I would never."

He reached out and his hand grabbed some delphinium, not yet ripe with flowers. "We need some green. Whether you intend to, I don't want you to encourage them. Do not forget that I control the voltages around your neck, and if I control them, I control you." He gave my neck a slight buzz to emphasize his point. "You will do as I tell you tonight, and nothing more. You will serve when I deem fit for you to serve, and there will be no resistance that I've grown to expect from you."

Did he know? He had to know. My heart was beating so damn fast I could hardly breathe. Delphinium. Larkspur.

I didn't want to draw attention to him, didn't want him to believe I was so oblivious to the world that I couldn't see what was happening in front of me. That I had no knowledge. They were just pretty flowers for an arrangement, after all. Just that. "That would be perfect. Maybe add some baby's-breath."

He smiled wide, believing he had forced me into cooperation. Forced into cooperation? Never would I comply. But scheme? Figure out alternatives? Find out how to take them all down? That I could do and I'd start with removing the control he had over me, start by getting this collar around my neck removed, deactivating it, not allowing them to have the power of pain to control me. Then? They all would be dead.

Despite what people believed, Warren did not like to take lives. Neither did Rex. But Ansel and I? Well, we basked in the feel of blood against our skin, and when I was finished with them, when I had the blood of every man in the room pooled and mixed on the floor, I'd be indisputably content. I was a trained assassin. Trained by the very man who cut flowers right next to me. But what he didn't train me for was weapons beyond the blades and knifes. He didn't train me for the art of creativity and the skills needed for thinking outside of the box. These were self-taught. They were well-honed. And now I had never been more appreciative of my search for knowledge.

I took a deep breath, trying to hide the sinister smile that threatened to overtake my expression. "There are some daffodils and I think some foxglove over there. What a lovely addition those would make."

He raised a single brow as he looked at me in surprise. "You know your flowers?"

"Just a little." *Do not smirk*. "A girl needs a hobby."

"Such an interesting hobby for such a rugged female like yourself."

"Yes," I agreed. "But I've always been one for floral arrangements."

"Oh, maybe you can help with it, then?" He was trying to be civil, but the fact remained—I was his captive. My life and the respect that I had offered to him meant nothing now.

"I'd like that." He had no idea what he was signing up for.

Chapter 11

REX

AN ILL LIT room greeted me when I opened my eyes. I closed them again, waiting for the dizziness that made my surroundings spin to settle. I fucking hate the effects of those darts. I'd like to hit them with a few hundred of them and see how they fared. I opened my eyes again, my vision set straight in front of me, while I wondered if I was hallucinating. I tried to move, but the chains weighed heavily against my skin. The rattle of the metal echoed in the room.

"The number of chains they have on you is overkill. What are you going to do? Snuggle them into defeat." Warren smirked, though I could tell he felt just as shitty as I did in this moment.

"Thanks for the ding to the ego," I muttered as I tried to blink away the grit. It took a few seconds for it to register that Warren was here, in this fucking cell, chains on every fucking inch of his body. And Ansel? I let my head fall to the side, seeing him completely out of it and equally subdued. "What the fuck got you here?"

"I could ask the same." Warren tried to lift his hand, but the chains prevented any movement.

"It was only supposed to be a fucking minute. She had promised." I spat the words out of anger, but I wasn't angry at her because it had only been about a minute when they attacked. "It's not her fault. I went willing. And it was only a minute in before they snuck to the window and got the darts into my body. She fought; I think. At least she had been when they finally brought me down."

"And the fire?" Warren licked his lips as he watched.

"What fire?"

"Both fires," he clarified.

"There were fires? What the fuck did I miss?" Shit. Thea hadn't mentioned fires. But then again, I was too focused on getting my cock sucked to listen if she had.

"The diner was up in flames when we traced you there. The cook said they took the omega."

I let my head fall back to the brick wall. If Warren was in his dragon form, this brick and chains wouldn't contain him. But he wasn't. He was a man, and though we may be mutants, our strength isn't as extraordinary as they assume. "Thea won't like that. They were friends."

"Of course they were. Our omega loves complications." I heard a soft groan coming from Ansel, but I didn't glance in his direction. "The apartment fire. Did Thea do that?"

There was a fire at the apartment? "I... I don't know. I tried to stay lucid, but you felt those darts. They aren't normal sedatives."

"She's here. I can feel it. I can smell her in the air." He paused as he listened to the noise outside our cell. "They had taken you to that facility as a halfway point, knowing we would follow and how easy it would be to trap us. Ansel was right, and I didn't listen."

"Never do," Ansel moaned before letting out a curse.

"What do we do now?" I asked because not once in all of our time together had we all been in chains at once.

Warren's eyes went to the bars. "We have friends, remember?"

Friends. Yeah, okay. Was that his way of saying Rodrick was on his way? Or was he hoping Rodrick would find us? "They had a strong interest in Thea. They didn't want her harmed. Odd, considering we are down here."

"They feared my wrath?" Warren wondered.

Footsteps echoed against the brick floor. I hadn't a clue where we were, but I suspected Warren knew. "Where did they take us?"

"Dungeons." His eyes looked at the surroundings, lit only by a sconce of fire mounted to the wall. "It was built into the White House from the minute this building was resurrected. I got caught as a child playing down here when I went to work with my father."

His eyes glazed over for a moment as he revisited a memory of what was no doubt a happier time in our lives. Before. It was all before the shots were administered to us and our lives were ruined. We didn't get a say in what happened to us. None of us did. But Warren? He had it the worst because his parents knew the possibility but had no choice but to let it happen. Others went into the circumstances blissfully unaware.

Keys rattled and brought our attention to the door. All of our eyes fell to the figure, though through the darkness and failing lights, it was nearly impossible to make out who stood there. When the door opened and a man stepped in, panic flooded me and my stomach tightened in fear. I had seen this man, just barely. His image was one of the last things that had filtered through my thoughts before I lost consciousness.

The barred door opened with an echoing squeak from years of never being oiled. His steps ground against the eroding floor, grinding the grit under each step he took. He stopped in front of us, his head going from side to side as he took in each of us and our appearances. It was easy for him to stand tall and proud when he wasn't contained by the weight of chains and stuck behind the bars of a prison cell.

"I see you all are awake." He smiled a smug smile that made me want to punch him. I wasn't the violent one, not normally. But the more time I spent around the jackasses who repeatedly threatened my mate and our well-being, the more I wanted to end them all. The time would come. They'd ensured their fate themselves. There was no way they could put us in chains and separate us from our mate without facing the wrath of the dragon. He was there inside of Warren, lurking under his skin. His eyes flashed with anger, his mind already thinking of ways to end this man.

"Where is she?" Warren asked, uncaring of his surroundings.

"Safe. Resting. I've given her a sedative to help." The thought of another drug in her system made Warren growl. "No worries. She didn't want it either, but her body needed to recover. We, collectively, as her staff, decided it was best."

"As her mate, I decide that it absolutely isn't for the best and I'll end your life for touching her." The words were spoken so harshly that I felt the ground under my feet vibrate slightly.

"Your kind is always so violent. What does that solve?" He shook his head slightly.

"Your kind sent hoards after us, knowing they would die. We may be violent but at least we value the life of our people," Warren shot back.

"They knew the possibility of death when they signed on for the job." He shrugged off the life like it was nothing. Shouldn't every life matter? Hadn't they realized that every life held something big? A bigger picture that one can't simply unravel just by a single glance. The pieces that fit and wound with the lives of others and the intricacy of it were astronomical.

"Their lives were equally important as your own," I stated, my brows furrowed in anger as I looked on.

"They are ants, and I'm the foot that crushes them."

"Who are you again?" Warren asked, verbally knocking him down a peg.

"A friend of Thea."

"That's a fucking lie. Thea doesn't have friends," Warren growled, and though that wasn't the full truth because I had met some people that Thea considered to be friends right before we were captured, in this case, I knew he wasn't her friend at all.

"I taught Thea all she knew. Trained her from a child," he said proudly.

I doubted he taught her everything. I'd known Thea a short time, but in that time, I've learned she was resourceful. I bet when she left his side, she continued learning, exploring, educating herself. I swallowed, my throat dry, then I spoke. "Keep your friends close and your enemies closer. Isn't that how the saying goes?"

"Essentially."

"Why?" Ansel asked. His voice sounded like sandpaper grating hard against his throat.

"She was an omega, but she had so much fight. We

used her. Not our normal experiment, but effective just the same."

"The others?" I asked, because I was genuinely curious. If she was an omega and they used her and that wasn't their typical experiment, what experiment did they normally do with omegas? Where were they?

"We'd collect them, then perform research. But it appears not enough research because we never could have predicted this outcome. Years we spent studying the mutants and their omegas trying to recreate something that you four did in just a few short weeks. Congratulations. To be honest, we are a little shocked and speechless."

I hadn't a clue what he meant. Apparently, neither did the rest of my family, because Warren pulled closer, his chains straining against his hands as he tried to force himself near the man. The look in his eyes was feral, and I wondered if he suspected something I hadn't yet connected. His jaw ground, his teeth gritted before he managed to say, "What. Do. You. Mean?"

The laugh out of the human was menacing. "Oh, I believe you know. We spent years trying to recreate natural life. Well, as natural as we could. Lab experiment after lab experiment, we had failed. An alpha and an omega aren't instantly compatible. Did you know this? How many omegas had you found before you stole our property and our most willing servant away?"

Warren's body flashed for a moment, bones stealing the place of skin before he settled back to the man. "No omegas. But I suspect you fucking know that since you've got them hoarded away."

"Oh." His brow rose, and he fell back on his heals, feigning shock. "Then this happened all by luck, then."

"What?" His fury was bubbling over. The ability to contain his rage was outweighing his logical thoughts.

Could he not see that this man, this mere human in front of him who thought his life was superior, was trying to get a rise out of him?

"The crossing of your group and our assassin."

"She's not your assassin any longer," Ansel pointed out.

"That most certainly is true. I believe she feels some loyalty toward you three." The admission was satisfying. "Our labs. They hadn't been able to recreate the dynamic you have. The outcome of trying to force matings has been unsuccessful."

"Speak clearly," Ansel demanded when Warren could not.

"We've not been able to create a child born between two mutants."

My throat felt like it was contracting. Trying to force words out seemed near impossible. "Are you saying..."

He waved me off, cutting my words off mid-sentence. "That you have. Yes. Amazing. Even more so, in the two days we've had her in captivity, the rate of growth is astronomical. There is no way to tell when this thing will come to term. There is no way to tell if it or Thea will survive. But, if so, our labs will wait, dying to study such a creature."

His declaration of ownership, his blatant disregard for us, our family, our ability to love, was repulsive. His admission of the plans they had with a child we created was intolerable. The chains containing Warren snapped one at a time as his neck bulged with veins and his face reddened with fury. The man in front of him licked his lips before slowly stepping back and shutting the door to the cell.

"I'd not worry. They are a prized possession at this facility as of now."

I inhaled, reining in the anger I felt that rivaled

Warren's and matched Ansel's. "She is not a possession. They are not a possession."

The man barely glanced at me before he spoke. "They are nothing more." He paused. "This does not mirror a human, and I never expected it to. Biology is not like that of a human any longer. But I'm expecting the results just the same."

Warren's growl caused the floor under my feet to shift and grit from the ceiling to billow down. He was seconds away from losing control and if he lost it now? There would be no saving anyone. He needed to stay calm. He needed to pull his dragon back so that we could work out a plan and figure shit out. He needed to—

"Oh, and boys?" A slow smile curved the man's lips. "We've got a fancy dinner tonight with the president. He's looking forward to catching up with his old friend. Behave. The omega will be there."

Like an emotional crash, the thought of seeing her again instantly brought peace. The circumstances? Not favorable. But I'd endure much worse if it meant seeing her again. It had seemed like an eternity from the moment she had ridden my body, not caring the guards were surely watching. It was a million years, a billion seconds, since my fingers had touched her skin. I craved it and I'd do anything to get it.

Not waiting for Warren to answer, I spoke over the rumble radiating out of him. "We'll behave."

I promised, not because I thought we wouldn't. But because I knew that no matter how much we behaved, our little omega absolutely wouldn't.

Chapter 12

ANSEL

I'D LIKE to say that the anticipation of a dinner party filled with finery and booze was at the top of our thoughts. But it wasn't. The only thing that even brought a remotely interesting aspect to this entire ordeal was Thea. That Thea was going to be there with us made my pulse instantly pick up. I could feel it thrum through my body in anticipation.

It had been hours since the man left. Hours since he dropped information at our feet, then walked out with a smug smile, looking so proud of himself. Hours since we all sat in silence processing our own thoughts, wondering if he spoke the truth or if he was baiting us for a reaction. He had gotten a reaction. He had nearly made Warren lose all control, but if Warren had snapped, it would have been the end of him. Warren would not justify saving a man who participated in the abduction of his mate.

Neither would I.

Since the moment his footsteps faded, I thought of

nothing more than driving a blade into his heart, slicing his throat wide open, severing arteries and watching his body bleed out. I wanted to feel the warmth of his blood ooze down my fingers, and when that happened, and it would happen, I wouldn't hide the joy that it brought me.

"He is lying." Warren finally broke the silence. "He wants to see us emotional. He wants to use our weakness to break us."

Though this may be true, I didn't think so. "I disagree." Shit. My voice was painful to use. Between the side effects of that dart that they shot into me point-blank and not even getting offered a sip of water, my throat was raw and burning. "He seemed genuine in his shock about the ordeal. Plus, things were changing with her. Fast. Her scent. Her internal makeup. I could sense it all."

"If what he says is true..." Warren let the words hang in the air.

"They would never get it. Not as long as we are living," Rex reassured him.

"We need a plan." I pulled at the chains that bound me before flexing my fingers that had long since lost all feeling. "Warren, you know this place. You know these people. What do you think they have planned?"

He let the silence hang over us for a moment. "It's a show of power. Clearly. The trap was set for us to be captured, and in my rage for my lost mate, I followed it. Even knowing it was a trap. If I had gone straight here, if her scent had led me to the White House, he knew he couldn't get the upper hand. I'd played on these grounds as a child. I'd sat in that man's lap and accepted candy from his palm. He knew, without a single doubt, that if I walked freely into this building, he wouldn't be able to stop me. We'd be able to hide. We'd catch them by surprise. But now? In chains... in chains, he could look me dead in the eye and gloat about my capture. Something he'd been trying to achieve for years."

The unspoken truth that none of us were saying out loud was that even though he prevented Warren from walking in here, that didn't mean that Warren hadn't shared the information. Rodrick's team was coming, eventually. Every tunnel in this place was mapped out, every secret entrance point that they tried to hide was known, and they may have us at the moment, but the captivity was short term.

"I don't think they intended things with Thea to get this far." I spoke. "She was sent to kill us, not make a family."

"If they had predicted this would happen, they would have sent our little assassin sooner. They've been hunting us for years, always barely missing capture. If Thea had been the key, they would have not hesitated to sacrifice her." I licked my lips. "I don't think they had any of this planned, and now they are just winging it as they go along. I mean, yeah, they planned to trap us to capture, but beyond that? This whole situation wasn't planned."

"I will not let them experiment on Thea. I won't let them hurt what's ours." I wasn't sure if he was referring to Thea being ours, or the bomb he dropped about a child. But if I was feeling protective, I couldn't imagine what Thea and Warren felt right now.

"They would die first," Warren growled.

I looked over at Rex, his body more broken and bruised compared to what they had done to us, and I was furious. Yeah, I knew they wouldn't hurt Thea, not in this state. But what had Rex done to them to deserve that? Existed. He existed, and because his life was a valid, living organism... they made him pay while waiting for Warren and me to show up. That alone meant that they would suffer.

"We need a plan." I muttered, mainly to myself, but the cell they held us in was so small the others couldn't help but listen.

"My favorite plan is staying alive." Rex looked at me with a single dimple in amusement.

"They said it was a dinner," Warren stated. "Which means that Mr. President wants to flex his accomplishment of having us all." He said Mr. President with such snark and mockery. "He wants us all to be forced to sit civilized while he brags. He needs us to know that he has the upper hand and he wants it to be clear that if we blink at the wrong time, he could hurt us, Thea, the child."

"We are in chains. What more gloating does the man need?" I questioned.

"He has a god complex. If he hadn't, do you think that we would have been created?" Warren looked at us. "He needs his ego stroked."

"The room will be guarded," I assumed. "He would have to know that he is in complete control. That means he can leave no room for us to challenge it. Guarding the room would make him assume we wouldn't dare to rebel."

"They don't know Thea, apparently," Rex added.

"They don't know Warren is angry," I chimed in.

"The fuckers are screwed." Rex's voice was sinister, because we all knew what was coming for them. Even if they went through all steps to stop what was coming and they were confident they were safe, Warren would prevail. He always prevailed. There was no way the humans could win unless they had a secret weapon that we didn't know about.

I swallowed the bile that rose. A secret weapon that they already clearly were holding over our heads. A child.

It was a disgusting fact, but true. They knew that there was no way Warren would do anything dumb. His need to protect would be in overdrive, and damn it, it was a fucking catch twenty-two. He was fucked if he did nothing and fucked if he didn't, and an understanding needed to be made in order for him to act.

"Warren," I began and then stopped, trying to think of the best way to say what needed to be said. With a hard swallow, I continued, "You have to do what's hard, you know that?"

"I always do what's hard," he stated, clearly confused.

"I meant if needed, you will have to pick between the two. Thea is what is important and I know that's hard to fully accept. I know your instincts all scream to put a child over your mate at this moment because they are one, but you realize that if you have to pick, you need to pick Thea."

"Impossible." Warren's displeasure caused the cell to shake and the chains to rattle.

"There will be others," I stated.

"We can't be positive." Warren's fury suffocated the room at the thought of what I had asked him to do.

"But what we can be positive about is that there will not be another omega for us. There will be no more mates. Regardless of what happens, pick Thea." Rex backed me up, and I was thankful for it. I knew that Warren's thoughts were pure caveman at times, and he couldn't fathom having to pick between the two, but this was all new to us. A life barely growing was fragile. The implications of any kind of mutation, shifting, even the strain of Thea pulling shadows could be detrimental to its growth and health.

Footsteps from a distance came toward us, so faint I knew I was the only one who can hear them. "They are coming. Please, Warren, do as I ask."

"I'm the alpha," he grunted.

"Then act like one," I snapped as the steps grew closer.

I didn't want to be an asshole, but I could play the role well. He was the alpha, the strongest one out of us. The leader of our bunch. But we have been working together long enough that without me on their side, on his side, his success rate wouldn't be nearly as successful. It seemed arrogant, but it was a fact. Sometimes, even when it was hard, Warren needed someone to speak truths and Rex wasn't strong enough and hard enough to do so. That left me and I refused to spare his feelings.

The steps stopped in front of the cells and a familiar scent drafted toward me. Familiar, but not recognizable. I took in a deep breath again, trying to distinguish the layers of it when a voice spoke. "We've come to collect you."

"You're filthy and you reek of disgust. It's a miracle that the president himself requested you." Another voice broke in. I opened my mouth, ready to speak my own witty comeback, when a bucket of ice-cold water crashed into us. The ice cubes bounced off our skins and clunk against the floor as the water fell to the ground. The echo as it flowed out of the cell through a drain in the floor filled the silence that was quickly consumed by a chorus of laughs. "Much better."

I shook my head, trying to clear some of the water out of my eyes since the use of my hands was not an option. "I'm sure your president would love the water staining his carpet and chairs."

I heard a curse, and I assumed the fuckers didn't think about that. Humans rarely considered the finer details. From the back of the group, a voice chimed in. "It will be fine. He'll hardly notice."

Hardly notice? I can't speak for Rex or Warren, but I was fucking soaked. Still, I said nothing more. The metal squeaked and groaned as they pulled open the cell door. The water splashed against my pant leg as they stepped onto the cement floor below my feet. They came toward us in groups, making sure we all knew that we were largely outnumbered. Why did it matter? We were weak from lack of food and water consumption, chained for our strengths, and had no way to even use our damn hands. How much of a threat could we be at this moment?

My mind went to Thea and her ability to manipulate the darkness with her mind, and I smirked. Apparently, a large threat to them. But me? I wasn't flying anywhere with these chains smothering my back, and my hands weren't holding a dagger, ready to slice someone open. Only... they were. I hadn't registered through all the commotion of people shifting into the small space, but a single tiny dagger had been placed into my palm. I inhaled again, trying to place the scent that was familiar.

Rodrick's man?

If he was, he wasn't known to me.

Still, I couldn't deny the fact that having something so little placed into my palm was a reassurance I hadn't had moments before. I forced myself not to react as multiple sets of hands grabbed onto my body. I clenched the small weapon, not letting on what I held in my palm. I didn't know the plan. I wasn't sure of what opportunity I'd have to use this weapon when my arms were tied behind my back, but I was positive that when the opportunity presented itself, I'd know.

They dragged Warren out first, and he didn't make it easy for them. Between his body weight, which was not light, and his unwillingness to cooperate, they had a struggle. But I knew it was only because a tired guard makes for a poor job. I wasn't sure if he had gotten the same treatment I had when it came to a hidden weapon. It didn't matter. His body was a weapon. But if you tire out the guards meant to stand at your back and knock you down a peg whenever they were ordered, they will be less prepared.

And when we were near, chaos always broke.

I went, Rex followed, and together we were trudged down a narrow hall, filled with people, to face the man that Warren had dreamed of going toe to toe with since the moment his family took their last breath. His time had come, and retribution had never tasted so sweet. Warren would make him pay. We all would. There was no price tag on the suffering we'd endured, but if I had to place a number on it, that number would be the president's life.

Chapter 13

WARREN

THE DAGGER that was slipped into my hand was confusing. I didn't know any of these men on this crew, and I wasn't completely certain they were mutants. But none of this mattered because it proved that people were on our side, and if they were Rodrick's men, then it only showed that our plan had been successful. Successful if you exclude that part of the plan where I dumbly walked Ansel and I into danger.

He's fine.

We're fine.

I can't fix the decision I'd made in the past, and fuck, I'd do it again even if I could. Because ... Thea. Thea was worth every damn thing that had happened since she walked into our warehouse, knife in hand, ready to slit our throats. Now that she carried our future, she was worth so much more. So much that even this fucking facility saw her worth. It wouldn't do. I refused to have this for her or our future.

I squeezed the small dagger in my fist, feeling the bite of pain as the blade cut into my palm. It was a refreshing reminder that I was alive and I'd a lot of fight in me. I'd buy my time waiting, seeking the perfect opportunity to strike. I'd strike hard, knowing that my entire team was behind me, ready to fight. In the meantime, I pulled against the chains, struggled against the hold of the man, making them work for every step we took down the hall. I wanted their energy drained. If their muscles weren't burning by the time we reached our destination, I hadn't done my job right. They needed to be worn the fuck out because if they were worn out? They wouldn't try to fight as hard when the time came.

Behind me, the boys had done the same, only their refusal was lacking and their fight was not nearly as hard as mine. Didn't matter. They needed to save strength, too.

I knew where we were going. I'd been there, in the exact spot, facing the same man many times in my life. I knew where I was going, but I wasn't prepared. I hadn't been prepared to walk into a room that had once held my father, standing tall and proud in front of a man who valued no one. I tried to hide the nerves that filled me, tried to hide the fear.

I was no longer a child.

I was a man.

A mutant.

A monster.

"It's been longer than I liked." A voice boomed from where he sat at the table. He stood. The man of my night-mares. The doctor of my own personal tragedy.

Dr. Donald Brass.

Mr. Donald Brass.

President Donald Brass.

I refused to give him the respect by calling him anything but what he deserved. Scum.

With my distraction, I let my fight die down. A hand gripped my arm as it dragged me toward the table. "Not fucking long enough."

"I would ask you to watch your tone. You are standing in front of our country's ruler." The guard who spoke slammed me into a chair, not bothering to remove any of the chains that bound me.

"Our country's dictator, you mean?"

"Enough," the former doctor roared. Or would it be current, since I knew he would never give up his experiments. When the room calmed and Ansel and Rex were placed in their own chairs, the doctor sat. "It's been a long time."

"Not long enough," I stated.

"Oh, come on now." He smirked as Thea entered the room. "Are you still angry I murdered your family?"

Thea gasped and though her hands were chained, they were in front of her, allowing her to cover her mouth. The president turned to her. "Hello, Thea, nice to meet you. I'm sure you know who I am. You could call me President or President Brass, whichever you prefer."

"She's not calling you any fucking thing," I growled.

He raised a brow. "The disrespect you have shown me is disappointing. Can't we let the past die?"

"Like my family?" I spat.

"Is it necessary to be so morbid? I honored you with this feast, and this is how you treat me?" He turned to Thea, then patted a chair next to him. "Thea, have a seat right here. Jerome, please take a chair as well."

I watched as my mate sat next to the man who had haunted my dreams for so many nights. The man who used the children of his employees as test subjects and slaughtered those who spoke against him. The man who single-handedly crumbled the government, then took it upon himself to grab the reins and control people, their thoughts, and the information they were fed. I closed my eyes, taking in a calming breath of air. It wasn't acceptable to be here with him, and I wasn't sure how long I could handle it.

The man who had once visited our cell, Jerome, sat opposite of Thea. He eyed us nervously as he spoke. "It should be noted that you will make no moves toward our leader."

"Stop me," I growled out the words, and with that, Thea's body seized.

In an instant, I began to fight against the restraints of my chains. The guards close to me stepped forward, taking hold of my body, pulling me down. I hadn't noticed it at first, but I saw it now. A thin band of metal that was locked tightly around Thea's neck, shocking her into submission. The remote? It sat proudly in the hands of the man sitting across from her. They disgusted me. I'd end each of their lives with pleasure. They knew they couldn't control us alone, so they had to threaten electrocution on her.

"As you can see." Brass's voice cut into my thoughts. "We have the upper hand here. We have the control. We could end her life at a moment's notice."

"You wouldn't." Ansel spoke. "She has what you've been trying to create, and us? We are the means to get there again."

He wasn't wrong in his assessment. They hadn't been able to get an omega pregnant. We had. If they kill any of us, they will lose so much potential research. It wouldn't get that far, though. I knew it. The dagger I clasped in my bound hands behind my back told me so. I just needed to wait, take in the room, figure out a plan. I eyed the perimeter of the room. It was large, and not a single foot of the wall remained without a guard. They feared us. The security present confirmed that. And they should fear us. We were long past the point of civil, and now we fed off the ruthlessness that had kept us alive for so long.

"You are correct," Brass confirmed. "I don't want to end your life. I'm curious how this process works."

Rex smirked, beaming his cheeky dimples toward Brass. "Well, it all started with a lot of fucking."

With a flick of his wrist, an order was placed, and a guard stepped forward, using a club into the back of Rex's skull. Rex, for all the pain that had to cause, didn't let his smile falter much as he leveled his eyes with the President of our country. They had a silent stare off, a small play for power, and though Rex was the meekest of our bunch, he didn't look away. He held strong in his will, proving that even the weakest of us was still stronger than the strongest, most powerful man they had.

Brass looked away first, turning his gaze toward Thea. "Thea here is going to be cooperative. Isn't that right?"

"I'll fucking kill you all," she gritted out, not caring that the words sent a controlled current through her body.

"I'll take that as a yes." Brass leaned forward, his eyes roaming over the food in front of him. "Help yourself. Eat." He smirked... "If you can manage."

He knew we couldn't, but he, Thea, and Jerome were more than capable of doing so. At first, Thea would not move, but offering food wasn't a suggestion. It was an order. Her eyes twitched with the current, and I fucking hated the power that the tiny remote had over her. A single button and she was at their mercy, doing as they pleased. She would slaughter them for this. There was no question about that.

Thea heaped on some potatoes on her plate and a side of salad before adding slices of roasted chicken. Luxury foods these days for sure and nothing like the just-add-water rations that so many people lived on now. It smelled delicious, but I knew its taste was nothing compared to the food the ladies in the kitchen in my community could whip up. She took a bite of the chicken, looking way, too aggressive for a girl who was about to get her stomach satisfied.

Brass cleared his throat. "Had Warren told you how we'd met?"

"No." She tried to keep her eyes off me, but for a single moment, they drifted in my direction.

"That's a shame. It was a lovely story, really."

"As lovely of a story as one can be when a man murders an entire family to keep his secrets." I ground my back teeth, trying to keep as calm as possible. It was nearly impossible when memories that haunted me for most of my life threatened to replay like a movie reel and there was no way I could stop them. I blinked my eyes, begging the memories to fade, knowing damn well that when I sat at the table with the monster who orchestrated the slaughter that haunted me, I would not truly escape the memory.

Thea's face displayed all the horror at my raw confession of my past. I hadn't told her because I hadn't wanted to see that face. I didn't want her sympathy. I would rather she assumed I was an unwanted kid, tossed on the street because I was different, than learn that I watched each of my family members die one by one as I hid in a tiny crawl space behind a vent.

"So far you hadn't told a soul, so as you can see, my methods were successful." He smiled fondly at me, and for a moment, I was transported back to a child, when the man in front of me, the true monster, dressed up as Santa, and I sat on his lap, confessing about the things I desired most. Times had changed. My desires had changed. And there was nothing I wanted more than to take everything he worked for, his position, his power, all his research, and let it go up in my flames of hatred. His attention turned to Thea again. "Thea, would you like to hear the story?"

I knew the question to her was rhetorical. I could tell by the glint in his eye that he was already set on turning my worst memory into a great tale for his entertainment. Thea opened her mouth to speak, but was cut off by his words. "I—"

"Long before the government crumbled, there was a lab built under this very building, the building that represents the free country and our government body. It was a secret place, guarded by the government, with the topmost lucrative projects coming here. We hired the most elite of employees and when they joined the ranks, they became family, their own families became our families. We believed in our mission and everything that our work stood for. That's how I met Warren." He eyed me while pointing at me with his fork. Bringing the fork to his mouth, he shoved the chicken into it and slowly chewed. When he swallowed, he continued with his tale, "His father was brilliant. Truly, he was."

"My father committed his life to your cause and look where it got him," I interrupted, fuming that he could praise the very man that he had killed.

"Sometimes, there are costs and casualties. He understood that. You should understand that, too."

Only I didn't understand that. Not when I'd spent my life paying a cost without a contract. I hadn't signed up for this, none of us who had our DNA altered had. We were innocent. Unknowing. Victims in the greed that this man had to create true power when power couldn't be created, it was earned.

"Warren's father worked under me creating a vaccine to cure the new deadly strand of smallpox that had risen. The old vaccine no longer worked. It had to be started from scratch and reconfigured." He leaned toward Thea, his chin resting on his fist as he fake-whispered, "Can I tell you a secret?"

"No." Her growl shook the china and champagne flutes in front of us, creating tiny vibrations of sound.

Brass only smiled. "There never was a smallpox virus that was unbeatable." My heart picked up its pace. I had never known this. I... Fuck, I thought my dad had really been trying to save the humanity he loved so much. "The smallpox outbreaks were all a hoax, creating mass fear among the people. Of course, my employees didn't know that. I did. I knew it all, planted the information, fed the media. I led them to believe they were doing the work of a humanitarian, but I knew differently. I wanted to see what it would be like to create what man was never meant to be. Day and night, I had people working on it. And the results, well, they far exceeded my expectations. Too far, if I'm being honest. I hadn't thought what I created would be so successful. It was too successful. The ramifications and fear caused the country to falter, collapse, not like it wasn't long overdue."

"Why are you telling me this?" Thea blinked slowly at the man in front of her. "I know the outcome of your disastrous science experiment."

"Warren was a rambunctious kid," he continued. "Always coming to the lab to help his father, always running around touching absolutely everything. Always so trusting." His gaze fell on me. "He was the first dose administered. Patient zero. Test subject one. Had he told you that much?"

Her throat bobbed as she swallowed. "No. He hadn't."

I kept my gaze ahead, not willing to look at Ansel or Rex. Unwilling to face the fact that I had hidden this truth from them. I was ashamed. I was a kid, yes. I had no control. But I was the monster that started it all. I was the first, the one who let this man who failed us all know that his dreams could come true, and I ... I'm an abomination because of him.

"It's true." He grinned. "His dad was hard at work, and Warren? Well, he was exploring places he shouldn't. I found him down in the cell room, the very one he had just came from. He had a ball in his hand, bouncing it about, and I swear if I close my eyes, I could still picture it like it was just yesterday. I told him he shouldn't be down there alone and we agreed to share a bag of Skittles from the vending machine. He followed me so willingly. Such a trusting soul. He got his Skittles, of course. I'm not a monster, but it cost him the injection first."

Thea gasped, and shame flooded me. Humiliation that I let myself get duped so easily by someone I trusted, and that because of my childish carelessness, I had become the monster that I am today. A freak. A mutant. An abomination. I couldn't look at her.

"That's enough."

My demand fell on deaf ears.

"It didn't work at first. Nothing. I waited a week and injected him again. Turns out it took a while for a full DNA change. The second injection was a mistake I would never make again. He was never meant to be that strong. None of them were. I lowered the dosages after that."

I dared to look at her, afraid of what I'd see. But when our eyes met, all I saw was anger. Anger not toward me, but for me. She took a calming breath, but it didn't calm her enough before she spoke. "You used an innocent child as your test subject. A child. A child who trusted you. If there was ever anyone more of a beast in this room than that man you've got chained up, it's you. You are the worst thing to ever happen to humanity."

"I'm a blessing to humanity. It was going to shit, anyway." Brass scoffed before continuing his story. "His father found out shortly after. It was something that couldn't be hidden when his child kept dramatically flashing between a human and bones as his body adjusted to what happened. He was angry, though he had no right to be. We had a marvelous contribution to put forth to this world. He didn't see it that way. He had threatened to tell everyone what the vaccination really was, out the hoax I had been feeding to the people, unravel the work I spent years developing."

"So you murder the whole family?" Thea was horrified.

"Clearly not the whole family, Thea. Warren is sitting right here."

"He tried." I spoke, my words so hard to push out of my throat. Was it closing up? Had I been poisoned some-how? Maybe in the water they dumped over my head? "He tried to kill us all. It was a Sunday lunch after church. My mom was a big believer. Turkey sandwiches, chips, grapes... the green ones with no seeds because I hated the red—our meal. I had soda poured into my glass, and we never got soda. Except Sundays. It was a reward for sitting through church service without incident."

"Warren." Rex tried to lean toward me, tried to offer comfort, but his bound hands made it impossible. "You don't have to speak."

"Let him finish. He's already started," Brass began, and he had the audacity to roll his eyes.

My eyes held Thea's. Telling this story made me feel raw, vulnerable, but I owed her the full truth about my life, didn't I? "My father heard a car door slam. He had already been on edge all weekend so he jumped up, checked out the window. I don't know what he saw. It didn't matter. He ordered my sister and I to hide. Find a good hiding spot, one no one would discover. I knew the perfect spot. We had played this game many times, though at the time, I hadn't really understood what my father was preparing me for. He only said sometimes, science and the men working inside had a cost. I think maybe he knew that whatever Brass was doing was deceiving, but he was afraid to speak up."

"I've never treated your father poorly." Brass raised his voice.

"You had him murdered. Can you be treated worse?" When he didn't answer, I continued, "Our house was older, with these big vents and crawl spaces. I crawled behind a vent, unseen, and watched. There was argument, at least yelling, but I didn't know what about." I paused as I shifted through the memories. What happened next didn't really matter in the end. "My sister's hiding spot wasn't as good as mine. She didn't make it either."

My eyes and nose burned with the story I had never once spoken, and it only fueled the anger inside of me. The dragon was awake. He was begging to come out, wanting to play, and it took all my strength to push him down. Brass clapped a hand together, tearing us out of our thoughts. "Now that Warren is done with his dramatics. Back to the vaccine, my serum. After Warren and a few other volunteers, we hit the poor hospitals, the hospitals that no one would remember seeing us at. The ones who only serviced the public for free and were littered with the homeless and single moms, trying to survive as well as they could. We distributed. We knew what we were doing. I won't deny that. I knew what it would do to this country, and I knew how I'd step up to it. I just hadn't fully realized the ramifications of having creatures I made roam the land."

"And what is that ramification?" Thea asked him. Her eyes burned so bright I knew she was struggling to not take control of the shadows in the room.

"I hadn't anticipated that each person would be so vastly different. When people of various weaknesses bands with those of strength, it complements their faults, and makes it harder to maintain control. I'd like to control my environment. Remove the threats. Create. It's why I need the omegas. I'm still a scientist at my core and I need to know what can be created and grow from my own creations. Omegas are weak. By keeping the weak among my creations, I can study them and learn, and start fresh. I'm clearly not out to kill all of your kind. I need some of you to experiment with. But I will not hesitate to kill what threatens my power. I will not hesitate to kill you."

Only, his claim was false. Omegas weren't weak. Omegas were the key to unlocking the power and strength to make us all unstoppable. My omega, sitting at the table, eating his food, was the biggest threat to his power he'd ever seen, and he was too asinine to realize it.

Chapter 14

THEA

WE SAT AT THE TABLE, guards around us. The man in front of me, the President who ruled our country since its infancy in its reformation, sat at the end of the table proudly. He had no regrets, and why would he? He had gotten away with the worst crime known to humanity. It wasn't murder, though that was on his list too, but messing with people, their lives, their beings... it was biological warfare. He had pumped our bodies with toxins, and used us as his weapon to crumble our country.

"I've never heard of you as a scientist," I pointed out.

He smiled, the smile sending a slimy feeling over my body. He disgusted me. If he hadn't before, he had as soon as I saw the broken look in Warren's eyes as he told the story about his childhood. I would have felt repulsed the moment I learned he took away the will of Warren by shooting him up with his questionable elixir without his parents' consent. No parent would have consented to that.

Not a single one that cared. Yet, he did so without an ounce of care or consideration.

"You think I would put my name out there so freely to take credit for this mishap? No." He laughed. "I blamed Warren's father, named him as the scientist behind it all, and who could dispute me? He was dead, after all."

I understood now. I got it. I understood why it was so important to Warren to take over control of this reformed country. Did he want a better life for mutants? I had no doubt. But a better life wasn't the whole reason he was set on overthrowing the government. He wanted to take everything from this man. He wanted to rip apart all he had worked for and leave him with the same void that was gifted to him so many years ago. He wanted to erase him and his existence for the history so that no one could ever speak a false word of greatness.

I clinched my fingers, balling them with the tension I felt. "You have no honor."

"I don't need honor." He tossed down his napkin. "I've got believers."

"They will know the truth." It wasn't a threat but a promise. A promise I knew I would fulfill if ever given the opportunity.

His eyes roamed over me, leaving my body feeling like it was layered in oil. "Jerome, care for some tea?"

I looked at my former mentor. "How much is he paying you? What is the cost?"

Jerome ignored me. He licked his lips, keeping his eyes on the President as he spoke. "Please."

"Thea. Would you care to serve us some tea? If you're good, I'll tell you about your sister."

My sister. My body stiffened; my heart raced. It was true. I had a sibling, and he knew all about her. I rose on shaky legs, taking steps toward the corner of the room

DELILAH MOHAN

where a buffet stood. On top of the buffet was a tray prepped for tea serving. Minus the hot water. I approached slowly, fearing that if I made any quick moves, I would feel the jolt of electricity coursing through my body again. It had happened too much, too often already, and I knew that if this collar was removed now, I'd surely have burn marks. I needed it off. That was my first concern. Once it was off, they couldn't control me. That fact was a tiny strand of hope I clung to.

"When I took your mother off the street, we had been watching you for some time. We knew what you were at that point, even if you did not."

I bit down on my lip hard, tasting blood. "And what was I?"

"An omega, clearly."

"Clearly," I mocked, but he didn't catch on.

"We tried to get you too, but... well... you were a slippery one."

I stopped in front of the sidebar buffet and flipped on the electric kettle. "My sister."

I sent the reminder because I knew he was getting off track. I did not need the reminder of how many times I'd evaded the law before I finally got brought in off the street. I didn't need him to reminisce about my past life experiences. I lived through them and they were rough, but I made it. He didn't take offense to my redirection, only continued. "I wondered. If a woman could breed one omega, would they all be? Of course, original DNA was a factor, but we took a risk. Interesting enough, it worked."

I didn't find that interesting at all. They used my mother as a lab rat and it was disgusting. "What happened to her?"

"Who? Your mother? She resisted too much," he stated.

128

Calming breath. Take a calming breath, Thea. I reminded myself that I could not kill this man with a collar around my neck. Not until the power behind it was removed. I took a spoon and dipped it into the loose tea, using the spoonful of leaves to fill a tea strainer. I let my eyes fall to the arrangement of flowers in front of me before looking behind me at the men sitting at the table.

Keep him talking. Distract him. "I meant my sister."

Even saying those words made me feel devastated to my core. I had a sister. I had a family. At least, I hoped I still did. I had been alone for so damn long and these men found me, my mutants, my new family. I couldn't be more thankful for that. But there is something on a deeper level, something that came from my very soul that wanted to have more.

"She's in a facility now." I reached up, taking the buds and leaves off what I had convinced my mentor to be just greenery for the setup. He had grabbed the greenery and some of the dried-out stems for color alterations. With a quick glance behind me again, I grabbed dried pods and put them into my pocket before stuffing the greenery into the tea strainer. He continued, and I struggled to listen, struggled to hear him speak over the sound of my pounding heart. "You've met her."

I stopped my movement, frozen in place. "Excuse me?"

"At the diner, don't you remember? She was there at the same time you were." At the diner. Bethany. Rex had mentioned she was an omega, and I brushed it off, maybe even feeling slightly jealous that Rex recognized what she was. "We collected her after you left."

I turned. "Where did you take her!"

I didn't mean it, I mean, I did. But I wished I had more control. The shadows pulled forward, darkening the room and before I had a chance to even realize what was happening, I was on my knees, electoral currents running through my body at a more powerful voltage than I'd previously experienced. Warren roared, smoke rising from his nostrils while all three of them struggled against the holds on them.

"Enough." The President's voice boomed. "You had terms, and you disobeyed. You knew the consequences. Get me my tea."

I struggled to my feet on shaking legs. If they wanted tea, I'd get them fucking tea. I reached forward, grabbing a few more Larkspur seed pods and breaking them open in my hand, before dumping them into the mix of tea leaves. For good measure, I pulled a few Foxglove leaves to add into the mix. When the kettle whistled, I reached over, picking it up, calming even as I imagined scalding the President's face with the hot water and watching his skin redden with pain. He'd deserve it. He deserved pain and suffering and so much more, and I doubt there was anything we could do to him that would suffice for what he had caused us all.

"Are you going to serve us or not, Thea?"

I poured the water into the cups, making sure the hot water ran over the tea strainers. The water seeped out in strands of brown, turning the liquid an earthy color. I picked up the saucers, carrying one in each hand as I walked toward the president first. I bent slowly, sitting it down in front of him, giving him a slight bow of respect that I absolutely did not feel. Then I carried the remaining saucer over to Jerome and placed it in front of him. He smiled wide, twirling the remote in his fingers as he toyed with my destiny.

"Careful, it's hot." I smiled broadly and wished they took a sip, anyway.

I read an article once where Larkspur was fed to cattle, and it took four hours to show signs of it. I didn't have four hours; I have now. One could only hope that the dose was enough, that the human body worked vastly differently at processing the gift. I took my seat across from Jerome. Every time I looked at him, all I could feel was disgust. Jerome Kent. I trusted him. I cared for him. He was the closest man I ever had to a father, and this was where it ended up.

Betrayal. The words tasted salty in my mouth as I whispered them. He didn't hear them.

My former mentor's attention was focused on the leader of our not so free world. "I'm going to propose a deal to you, Thea."

I didn't want to do a deal with any of them, but as Kent picked up his tea and sipped it, I knew I'd buy time any way they could. "Please, explain further."

"You behave. Let us monitor you and the child." The child, the thought, still made me cringe. I felt both confused and oddly protective. "And when it's over with, I'll bring you your sister."

The conversation progressed slowly, painfully so. Still, the tea was left untouched in front of the president while Jerome had finished the whole cup. I waited. Anticipation gnawed at me. I hoped it would work. There was no reason not to. I tried to avoid my men's gazes, sure that if I made eye contact with them enough, one of them would break, and if that happened, my plan would be spoiled.

The sun that shined through the windows showed it was near dusk. Why were we even here? To flaunt his power and control? We knew it all. About his research. His facilities. He even told us all the governmental plans he had, and each time he spoke, I despised him more. He truly was the worst in humanity, and maybe Warren and I wouldn't be great leaders, but that was okay. No matter how awful we were, we had to be better than this.

"Thea." I snapped back to reality, unaware that I had been spoken to. "I asked you to serve dessert."

I blinked a few times, trying to clear my thoughts. The bigot belief that a female was only useful in serving men made me wrinkle my nose in disgust. He created a society that reverted to old fashion, completely outdated practices, and I would not adhere to them. They needed to go. There were so many things in this new government that needed fixed, and I couldn't help but think that if we died here, my people, both mutants and women would never flourish.

The slight buzz at my neck reminded me I didn't have the luxury of refusing to serve them. One word of disagreement would land me crumbled in pain on the ground and my energy zapped from my body. I eyed my mentor, and I hoped he could read the disdain in my glare before I pushed my body out of the chair. My steps were slow as I walked toward the buffet table. It may not be a lot of time but fuck, I was going to buy myself any moment I can in prolonging, praying the Larkspur hit their systems.

"Thea." I stopped mid-step and turned my attention to the president.

"Yes, sir?" I tried to sound as innocent as possible.

"Is there a reason you are not moving with haste?"

The only reason I wasn't moving with haste? Because I wished for the men in front of me to collapse with paralyzing and utter fear when they realize what I'd done to their drinks. No. No real reason for walking so slow. I licked my lips and widened my eyes innocently. "I'm just feeling awfully tired. It must be ..."

I trailed the words off and let them fill in their own blanks. I knew the conclusion they would draw. That conclusion would be false. Whatever child they thought I was carrying had absolutely no effect on me at this moment. It was a cell, and I didn't care how much they thought it was rapidly growing. I had yet to see the signs of it.

"The child. Of course." He turned to Jerome. "Make note of the time and symptoms. We'll enter it in the data base later."

"I don't think that's necessary. I wouldn't want to inconvenience you with this small act." I acted like I didn't want to inconvenience them, but I would inconvenience them until the day I died if they didn't let me go free. They would have no choice. I'd always win even if it were insignificant victories.

From the far side of the table, Warren raised a single brow in question, secretly calling me out on my bullshit without speaking a single word. He understood though, with this collar on my neck, it was all a game to them, and in return, it would be a game for me. Jerome cleared his throat and pulled at his collar as the president spoke. "In science, it's best to log everything, even the insignificant. If I hadn't, you wouldn't be where you are today. Please log it, Jerome."

Where I was today? He means a freak to society? An outcast? Family-less? Struggling to live a life that was only meant to be successful if you were like him, a man. A regular, non mutation, man. Jerome opened his mouth to speak, the words seeming hard for him. I tried to hide the smile. "Yes, s-sir."

I picked up a pie slicer. Not my normal weapon of choice and stupid of them to trust me with it, but it would do. After taking out a few plates, slicing some apple pie and plating them to serve, I used the tablecloth to wipe off the surface before placing the serving tool into my shirt and tucking it in place using my waistband. I grabbed the plates, one in each hand, and turned toward the President. I walked slowly toward him.

When I reached where he was, I bent at my knees, placing a plate of pie in front of him. "Sir?"

"That will be fine," he confirmed.

I turned and rolled my eyes. I hoped he choked on it. I walked toward Jerome and smiled charmingly. His brows were coated in a sheen of sweat, and the rise and fall of his chest seemed to have sped up. I placed the pie in front of him and smiled sweetly. "Enjoy."

He only looked at me, his eye twitching. When he made no move to take a bite of the pie, President Brass issued his order, "Eat the pie. It was freshly baked this morning."

I sat down in front of Jerome and watched. His hands struggled to reach up, his movements were stiff. His fingers struggled to grab the fork for a moment. When he had the fork in his hand, he scooped a piece of pie off the plate and slowly brought it to his mouth. Half the pie fell from the fork before it reached the destination. He opened his mouth and shoved the pie in. That was as far as he could go. By the time the pie made it to his mouth, the poison was already too deep in his system and the paralyzation was setting in. He couldn't chew, though, for a brief second, he sounded as if he was going to try. Then, instead, a choking sound escaped him.

"What are you doing?" President Brass demanded. Jerome didn't answer; his face turning red, oxygen unable to reach his system. "What did you do?"

The President's eyes were on me accusingly. I shook my head innocently. "I don't know what you mean, sir."

"What's happening to him?"

"It appears he's choking," I pointed out. Or dying a death brought on by Delphinium. Poisoning by Larkspur wasn't a pleasant way to go. It caused near-muscular paralysis and it could lead to respiratory failure, though he never would get that far. His cause of death would be brought on by me as he sat, knowing that the poison that ran through his system was the same poison he willingly cut off the plants for the hideous flower arrangement.

"Do something," the President demanded, and well, he gave me an order.

In a blink, I stood with a butter knife in my hand. I didn't hesitate to sail the knife forward, putting so much weight behind it that the impact as it impelled itself into Jerome's skull meant nothing but a sudden death. His body dropped, the remote that controlled the collar falling to the floor and skidding toward Rex. I couldn't think about the remote, it was too late for that. Before any of the guards around the room thought to react, I had the pie cutter out. I flicked my wrist hard, aiming for a guard next to Warren.

He was the strongest here. If he were to be free...

The serving utensil hit the center of the guard's chest. In seconds, Warren roared. The chains that bound him snapped and fell loudly to the floor before he jumped up, with a tiny weapon I hadn't known he possessed in his hand. He slammed it into the guard on his other side. Then he reached for the handle of the server. With a hand on each handle in the guard's chest, he pulled them down, dragging them through the guards' bodies until blood poured out onto the table, followed by the sickly wet sound of their intestines slipping from their body.

Warren's eyes found mine, and for a moment, all was still. Then a slow grin curled his lips, and all hell broke loose.

Chapter 15

WARREN

I DIDN'T KNOW what Thea was up to, but I knew she had to have something planned because never had I seen my mate so damn compliant. Sure, having a collar around her neck could have something to do with it, though I doubted that to be true. She had way more fight in her to let a simple collar subdue her, even if it looked painful as hell when she fell to her knees at a single press of a button. I nearly lost it when I saw that. Ansel and Rex had trouble controlling themselves, too. Still, she got up and served the scum in front of her like she hadn't just had her life flash before her eyes.

She was strong like that, my glorious mate. My omega. My complete and utter downfall.

I watched her every move closely and when she delivered the tea, her eyes repeatedly falling to the cups, I knew right then that Thea had a plan. I watched, and I waited, knowing that our time was coming. I loosened my chains, regularly stretching them out with my strength until I knew the metal had grown weak, and if too much pressure was applied, they would snap. When the man sitting across from her, Jerome, sweat profusely, I knew our time was coming. His heartbeat changed and I could hear the panic set in.

It wasn't until the first weapon flew, a single, dull butter knife, that I knew it was time. I didn't need a moment more than that, and Thea knew it. The pie cutter sailed through the air and impaled into the guard next to me. I stretched my limbs, pushing at the chains until they snapped, falling noisily to the ground at my feet as I stood up. Without hesitation, the tiny blade that was put in my hand was plunged into the other guard at my side. I took hold of the pie cutter handle and, together with my blade, I pulled downward. The blood of both men oozed over my palm and I'd never felt more at home.

The further I dragged the blade, the more their bodies gaped until their insides spilled out, no longer held in by their skin and muscles. With a last gasp, both men stumbled, their bodies dropping to the floor like sacks of flour. A roar of satisfaction left me, though I hadn't gotten to enjoy the satisfaction for long. I bent down, pulling out the pie cutter and knife, waiting for whatever came at me.

From a few seats down, Rex flung his head back, knocking it into the guard that restrained him. He struggled the few steps, with arms pulling him back, but he made it to the remote that had controlled Thea's collar. His foot stomped down, hitting the remote repeatedly with such force that after only a few blows, pieces of it skated across the ground, shattering its effectiveness. That was all Thea and I needed. Without their ability to control her, she was free to act as she pleased, and I was free to do the same.

I didn't hesitate to open my mouth and inhale, sucking in the soul of the nearest guard as another tried jumped on my back. I flung the body of the man off me, not bothering to eat his soul but opting to drive my blade into his heart. The twist as I tore apart his most vital organ was satisfying. If only I had the chance to enjoy it. Outside, commotion broke, and I knew, or at least hoped, that the commotion was Rodrick and not reinforcements heading this way.

My eyes roamed the room. The guards were moving in. Their bodies moving slowly as they debated which of us was the least of a threat. Joke's on them. Both of us were equally deadly. I let my eyes fall to the empty chair, and a roar left me. The President, a fucking coward of a man, was nowhere to be found. He would die, I'd make sure of that. For me, for Thea, for all that he had done to us all. I'd find him, and his life would end.

"Where's Ansel?" Thea muttered, though her voice held panic.

I didn't see him move. I should have, but I was preoccupied with my thoughts, too worried about the men closest to me to worry about the ones who were a part of me. "He's gone. Where the fuck did he go?"

It was a rhetorical question. Not even one of us knew the answer to it. Nor were we allowed to ponder it long. The first man charged toward me and he was fast, faster than I would have thought for a human. Faster than I'd seen, and for a moment, I wondered if it was more than DNA that was being altered in this facility. What else had Dr. Brass, our beloved president, done to the people? The guard plowed into my stomach with a force that nearly left me winded. I recovered easily enough, getting my hand into the strands of his hair and pulled him off me. His body was light, and he dangled from my grasp, his toes barely grazing the ground.

His hands reached up, his fingers finding my face. His thumbs went for my eyes. I tilted my head back, allowing my mouth to open as I sucked slowly. I let his soul peel from his body, one strand at a time, as he howled in agony. Each tiny pull of his soul leaving him fed my dragon, satisfied by his need for brutality. The man and the dragon weren't so different. Both got a thrill of pleasure from the suffering of the man.

The surrounding room darkened as I dropped the body from my grasp. Thea was at my side in moments, Rex not far behind her as he twisted off the rest of his chains. It was us, three against the room, and the occupants in it had their eyes locked on us. I had no fear. I couldn't. Thea was by my side, and even if she still had that collar snug against the skin on her throat, I knew Rex had destroyed the remote. Nothing controlled her; therefore, nothing controlled me.

She didn't hold back. The moment she was free of control, she let her shadows rush around us. They slinked against our skin, and when they touched us, I heard a slight purr of content vibrating through them. But that was impossible. They weren't alive. Yet, nothing really seemed impossibly any longer, not with Thea by my side. The mystical omega that we thought we'd never meet. How could anything go wrong now that we were bonded together so strongly?

The shadows danced in front of us as guards advanced, forming a wall of protection. She turned to me, her eyes burning with intensity. "We need a plan."

I knew she was holding them off. That those shadows she held in front of us were keeping the guards away, but it cost her energy that she couldn't afford to burn. I glanced around. I had no fucking idea what we were to do, but we were outnumbered and surrounded. They had planned for a resistance; they would have been stupid not to. It was the reason the walls were lined with so many guards, waiting to take us down, and now it was their time to shine. How naïve they must be to think that they could overpower us so easily. What lies had Mr. President told them to have him hop forward so hopefully, thinking they would be the ones to take down the mutants?

"Did you see where Ansel went?" I asked.

"No. He was just gone."

I licked my lips, looking around suspiciously. How convenient for the man that appeared most vulnerable to have disappeared from our sights at the same time as the president. Only little did they know they grabbed the wrong one. If they wanted vulnerable, they should have taken Rex. Ansel... he was more sufficient than I was in most cases. "We'll worry about him later." I watched as a man bounced off the shadow after running full force toward it. Thea had grown stronger, and it made me so fucking proud. "He can handle his own."

She nodded her chin toward the men that were struggling against the wall of darkness. "And them?"

"One at a time, Thea. Drop the wall, let them come. Let us prove to them what the action of a genuine leader looks like. We would not cower down under threats. We will stand our ground and show them how strong we can be."

Thea didn't speak, but turned to the wall of black and let it fall. The first layer of guards fell forward, not expecting the wall to give. They tumbled down to their knees, making themselves vulnerable. Thea raised her hands, her arms wide, before she clapped her palms together. The shadows came fast. The men hadn't even stood up before the force of the unseen smashed into them, applying so much pressure as it squished their bodies together that they couldn't breathe. The impact was so great they could barely gasp as their organs were squished and flattened.

As blood pooled in their mouths and dripped down and their ears were ripped apart, I looked over at my mate. She was mad. Terrifying. So fucking beautiful that I couldn't wait to be done with this mess and start our life together. Forever. Free.

When the last of the row of guards collapsed dead, she released them. The row of men behind them looked on in horror, and they should have been afraid. They should have been afraid long before now, but either they were too brainwashed to realize it or too damn stupid to care. I stepped forward as Rex's skin shifted and changed, blending in as he went along the backside of them. His presence was undetected. They focused only on me and Thea. Each step I took forward, they stepped back, until there was no room to step without stepping into Rex.

I knew he hated this part of our lives, knew that he wasn't the killer among us. But I also knew that above all, he put Thea above his wants and needs, and these men aided in her danger. They abducted them and stole their security. They abused him without a warranted reason. Rex's eyes took on an ethereal glow as he reached forward, grabbing the first man who bumped into him. His arm wrapped around the man's neck as he pulled the man toward his chest. The blade that sliced into his neck was quick. The body dropped as Rex reached for the next, no longer caring about who was harmed, as long as we were out on top of the situation.

I opened my mouth, letting a roar escape me before I inhaled, sucking in whatever soul was nearest to me, tasting the oily sweetness as it slid effortlessly down my throat. My dragon hummed its approval as it slid around under my skin. The souls fed his strength, and he was dying to be let out to play. I wouldn't let him out, at least not yet. Not after how hard it was to return him the last time, but it was comforting to know that he was there, like an extra layer of protection, ready to protect what was ours.

Thea was an unstoppable force, her will to fight unmatched. Her aim, impeccable. Her deadliness, nearly ninety-nine, perfect accurate. She had no hesitation as she used anything that could impale a body and drive it into her enemies. Not a single flinch as blood spurted up, coating her skin and dripping into her eyes. She was a warrior. A goddess. A queen in a red coat. Nothing could stop her, and if they tried...

A man jumped from behind her as another aimed low, trying to knock the wind out of her and make her motions halt. She spun fast, driving the end of a spoon into one man's neck before opening her mouth and...

The soul left the man effortlessly. Floating in a wave toward her until it disappeared down her throat. She swallowed before her mouth opened again and a stream of fire released, burning the flesh of the guard closest to her. She just... Fuck, my mind couldn't compute. She had taken on a piece of my dragon and used his strength flawlessly. Wrong place, wrong time, did not stop my cock from growing hard watching her or a smile to spread across my face. She was perfection, and she was mine. Ours. She was ours.

We thinned the room out fast, each of us forming a point of a triangle, the points all equally deadly. They had no way in, no way out. The only certainty they had was the death that one of us would deal with them, and if they were lucky, it would be quick. Most weren't so lucky. Most weren't gifted with the satisfaction of an instant departure. Most withered and screamed as their blood coated our skins, and they cried, knowing the last thing they saw was our sinister smiles.

But all of them, every one of them, left this earth while their bodies remained in a pool of their very own blood.

Chapter 16

ANSEL

THERE WAS A DISADVANTAGE, I supposed, to having one of my senses removed. When Thea threw her first weapon, I heard the whoosh as it broke the air. After that? The sounds became too much, too overwhelming to filter through. There were too many movements, heartbeats, and by the time I had filtered through them and rose, ready to aim at the nearest threat, it had been too late. The arm was tight around my throat as it wrapped around me. The weapon in my back didn't waver as it was jammed into my spine, and I knew that to move would risk my life.

I needed a plan.

I always fucking needed a plan these days.

The arm pulled me backward while chaos played strong through the room. The move pulling me away from the sound until it was gone completely. I clung tight to the dagger in my hand, the one that was placed there by what I assumed to be one of Rodrick's men. Only the person who placed it disappeared soon after, his heartbeat drifting away the first chance he got.

My heels dug into the floor, trying to halt the movement. It didn't help. If I hadn't had the chains, things would be different. But I wasn't as strong as Warren. I couldn't just break them. I hadn't had the ability to maneuver my body like Rex, so I couldn't flex and bend until my arms were around the front, making it easier to ditch the setup. I had wings. That was my strength of a mutation, and I couldn't even extend them at this moment.

"You're not the one I wanted." A voice, one I recognized as the president's, broke through the sounds of me struggling and the heavy breathing of the guards that tried to restrain me. "But I bet he will come for you, and that's all that matters."

I was confused. What was the point of it? He had who he wanted. Why did it matter if he came for me? "Did your dinner party not go as planned?"

"I will admit, I hadn't expected the omega to be so bold. I wanted to get a feel for your group together, see how you interact. I hadn't thought there would be disruption."

That oversight was on him, then. Of course, there would be a disruption. He held four mutants captive. "What did you expect?"

"Peace. I wanted to make Warren an offer." His footsteps were loud against the tile, and the smell of expensive cologne made me bite my lip to prevent gagging.

I tried to pull my arm free, but the grip was too tight. We were down. Lower into the building, maybe into the earth? "An offer?"

"I'd give him the omega back, unharmed after the child. But in exchange, I want his cooperation to let me experiment on him. Now I know what you're thinking, he's here, I could do it anyway and that may be true. But how much easier would it have been to have him do these things willingly, without fighting and guards and all the death and blood that he seems so fond of?"

If he thought Warren was so fond of death and blood, he'd never really spent time with our omega. "And the child?"

I asked, even deep down, knowing the truth. He didn't need to speak it for me to know his plans. Still, he answered anyway, "Oh, that will be mine. That is not up for negotiation."

I wasn't sure what type of delusional world this man lived in, but he had to realize that there would be no way Warren or Thea would agree to that. "Kill me now because if that is what you're negotiating over, you won't succeed."

"You place too much value on what hasn't come to fruition yet." Metal groaned against solid flooring, and I suspected a thick steel door opened. I could smell the steel as we passed before we entered a room that smelled like sterilizing antiseptics. The temperature dropped, casting the room in an uncomfortable chill.

A few feet more and my body was slammed down, forcing me to sit in an icy metal chair. President Brass's words played in repeat in my mind until the meaning clicked. "Are you saying that you would abort the child without their consent?"

"I don't need consent. I'm the president, remember?"

I blinked a few times. "Consent is basic human right."

"Except you aren't humans." He spoke so quickly that I knew he believed that. Maybe not fully, now. But once, we were born a human, too, just like he was. The only difference is we were victims of his science experiments.

"What was the point of leading us to Virginia?" I wiggled my hand against the chain, trying to remember the tricks I had seen in the past.

"If Thea was there when Warren arrived, he would have destroyed us all to get to her before we had him contained." A clink of metal and a cabinet opening drew my attention, putting me on high alert. What had he planned? "I couldn't have that. If I let him come here, he would have known where to find them. He's been here many times over and a kid always finds the places he shouldn't be roaming."

"He will know where to find me, then." I shrugged.

"He won't get past the guards." He seemed confident. It was ill-placed. "I have the best in there. Well trained for this situation."

Had he not known? Did he not hear the team outside or the scuffles that were beyond the building walls? Or was he just so confident in his actions that he didn't fear them as threats? "So what? When you have Warren and Thea contained again, you expect them to be brought here?"

"It's clear that civility is not something we can obtain. He needs to see what's at risk." The snap of latex gloves had my pulse quickening. The sound of glass clinking made me fight the urge to move nervously. "I had tried to play nice. You were there, you saw it. Still, he disrespected me."

Tried to play nice? By gloating about his retched accomplishments and dragging up horrendous memories of Warren's past, forcing him to tell it all while he internally relived the fear of a child? How was that playing nice? "Respect hasn't been earned. Surely you know it works both ways."

"It's a matter of opinion. I am the leader of this country. Have you forgotten?"

I smirked. "I've never seen you rule."

I thought I was funny speaking the truth. He did not. The back of his hand sailed across my cheek so quickly I hardly heard it coming. His knuckles met my skin, clashing my cheek into my teeth. The metallic taste of blood flooded my mouth and mixed with my saliva. Externally though, I didn't even flinch. I let the mix of blood and spit build in my mouth before I spat it at his feet. "You hit like a girl and I don't mean a girl as powerful as Thea."

"You insult me, yet you're the one in chains," he said proudly.

"I think when you chain up a blind man and have him outnumbered by guards, you can't really gloat about how successful you are." I tried to shrug my shoulders, though the chains made it impossible to move more than an inch. "It's pathetic, really. You're not strong enough to do the job yourself, so you've got to have your goons do it."

"Strong enough?" He laughed. "God, no. I've never been a fighter. Powerful enough, though? Was it not clear that I have all the power a man needs and I'll wield it at my whim?" He cleared his throat. "I've been doing a lot of experiments over the years. Trial and error. I've had lots of hypotheses and failed conclusions. But want to know what I've discovered?"

I wished at this moment that my eyes could see. I strained them, trying to make out dark moving shapes and movements. It was impossible to decipher what was happening. I couldn't see what he held in his hands. I couldn't alert myself to a danger that wasn't visible to me, but in my gut, I knew that danger was near. I licked my lips, the skin dry from dehydration. "What have you discovered?"

"Nine out of every ten mutants who receive a second dose as an adult die."

I swallowed hard. "And the one?"

"Has to be killed because it's so monstrous we can't let it live without fearing for the safety of others."

"And Warren?"

"A fluke. He was a fluke. The records had been lost, I assumed. Stolen by his father and destroyed, and because of that, I can't seem to replicate it. I can't seem to get the dosages correct, the exact formula I used on him. I hadn't had a chance to make the formula in bulk before the specifications disappeared. I used what I had before I realized the mishap. It doesn't matter. It seems it's only children that take well enough to the second dose. But, even then... it hasn't ended well enough."

"You've been testing on children?" My mind entered a state of fury while my body remained relaxed. Was this what he wanted to do to ours? Test on her? Use her as a lab right to get his ideal dosages just right. *Her.* Because deep down, I knew our child would be a little omega, just like her mother. And after what he had created and stored ran out, had he been spending all these years trying to recreate the exact formula?

"Not important ones."

A rubber tourniquet was tied around my arm, the sudden pinch of my skin causing me to flinch.

I couldn't pull away; I wanted to. I wanted to put as much distance between me and him as I could because, at this point, I knew exactly what was about to happen. I'd be another trial and error. Another attempt to adjust the doses. Another possibility of failure. "How does it feel?"

"What?" The president's movement paused.

"How does it feel to have taken all you ever wanted, stolen all the control of the surrounding people, and still have failed?" I needed to buy time. I needed to get my hands free. I needed to get out of this fucking mess.

"It feels victorious. You'll see."

I wiggled my arm. "Wouldn't it be easier to unchain my arms? It can't be easy to get at my vein from that angle."

If I could just get free, I'd show him exactly how powerful a sightless mutant could be. The guards first. They were my main priority. They hovered on both sides of me like pillars, waiting for me to misbehave. But they were lax, not seeing the threat in me. Underestimation could be deadly. I just hoped they got the chance to find out.

"It would be easier, but I don't trust you." His voice was low, spoken from a distance as he gathered his supplies.

"No worries." I acted carelessly. "I just figured, at least from what I know, the serum goes into the bloodstream. I hadn't had a drink in at least twenty-four hours, so dehydration is sure going to make getting at these veins a fucking bitch."

"I hadn't thought of water," he mused. Of course, he hadn't. That would be a human decency thought, and we did not deserve the decency that everyone whose DNA hadn't been fucked deserved. "Release his chains, but keep your grip on him tight."

I tried not to smile, tried not to show the sinister glee I felt as the adrenaline kick in. Knowing that in moments, the calm would be broken and bodies would lie at my feet caused me an unnatural satisfaction. The chains tightened against my skin before they slacked, allowing me to shake free of the restraints. I shook my arm, coaxing some feeling into it. I waited until the uncomfortable tingle coursed through my limb before I brought an arm forward, leaving the other arm with my dagger behind my back.

I wasn't ready to give away my weapon just yet, wasn't about to announce that I'd be ready to pierce their skin in a moment's notice now that I was free of the restraints. I waited as the hands that held my shoulders down relaxed some. Their grip subtly loosened. I waited, anticipating, as the gloved fingers of the president pushed against the inside of the arm. And when the tiniest drop of liquid spilled onto my skin from a needle that hovered over my limb, I unleashed the beast he created me to be, and struck.

Chapter 17

REX

IT WAS A DISASTER. Everything was. This wasn't how any of this was supposed to go. How did going to Thea's apartment for one thing end with a pile of bodies at our feet and blood coating my hands? I'd never get clean of it, though I prayed the metallic scent of it faded off my skin and only remained a memory. The last body had fallen to Warren, his body tortured and bent unnaturally before his soul was pulled from its encasement. The pristine white walls were now painted red, spattered unevenly with the blood of men.

I was dazed. Confused. So damn tired. How had we gone from a nice breakfast before the sun rose to this? A bath of blood on the White House's marble floor.

The double doors to the side opened, and a body fell through, landing right in the middle of the pathway. Seconds later, Rodrick appeared. He looked between all of us, still positioned in a triangular formation, and nodded approvingly. "Y'all seemed to have had some fun."

"I mean, it was no game of Monopoly, but we won." Thea smiled as she spoke. The blood that smeared her face made her look every bit of the deadly assassin she was.

Rodrick's eyes roamed. "Where's Ansel?"

That was the question of the fucking hour. Where was he? I knew exactly who he would be with when we found him and that was about to become our number one priority. Warren reached down and grabbed a napkin that had fallen to the floor, the piece of material strangely untouched even as the table that once divided the room remained in pieces and the fine china charred through the room, now rendered useless.

Warren wiped his hand on the napkin, changing the cloth to a disgusting shade of red and copper. "Brass took him. We didn't see it happen. But I know where to find them."

A nod was all Rodrick offered. "Then lead the way. We'll follow you anywhere. Never doubt that."

Rodrick's men agreed. Warren's lips curved up as he looked at Thea, no doubt thinking the same thought I had. "We'll get Ansel, we'll take the presidency, and after, we'll find the omegas."

Like a choir, each of them whispered the word omega with awe in their voice. I doubted any of them truly believed Warren's promise. But we'd prove them wrong. We knew they were out there and, well, we'd find them. All of them. Every omega would be free. My eyes met Thea's and held for a moment, the intensity nearly too much for me not to look away. We'd free all the omegas, or we'd die trying.

Warren walked toward the double doors, stepping over the dead carefully, as if their blood and gore hadn't already covered his boots. When he reached Rodrick, he pushed past him. We followed, knowing that if anyone could find Ansel, it would be Warren. We reached the end of a hallway when he turned to us. "He will have it guarded. Be ready. Keep your eyes and ears peeled. Brace yourself for whatever chaos he would like to continue until his death. He has a god complex, so he doesn't think we can kill him. But we can. We will. And we'll prove to everyone just what an awful being they followed so blindly." Warren turned his back to us all, trusting us with his life as he pressed into a wall, searching for some sort of hidden mechanism among the white marble and crisp walls. "My father used to enter this way sometimes. It was to be kept closed during business hours, but at times, he had to take the shortcut."

I knew the words about his family were meant for Thea and I. No one else mattered when sharing the truths but us and we'd already learned the most horrific details of it. We'd already listened to the horrific experiences he'd lived through and learned just how much his family had cared for him, what they would have done for him, if the man the country looked up to as a leader hadn't murdered them.

A slight push of an indent in the wall made a click echo. The rush of air as the door popped free blasted against my skin before he pulled the swinging door fully out to reveal a set of stairs. He didn't look back as he stepped inside, his body disappearing down the steps before Thea and I could even think about following him. Thea went next, her dark hair flowing behind her in a tangled mess as she entered the gray cement stairwell. I entered, leaving Rodrick and his men to take our tail. I didn't want to split up from my family. If they went down, we went down together. Wasn't that how it should always be?

The stairway was dark, faintly lit by flickering fluorescent lights as we descended into the underground, heading into the unknown. Warren held a finger up to his lips when we reached the end of the stairway. He peeked into the tiny square window, eyeing the threats that remained out of view because of the door. When he was done, he leaned back, his voice a whisper. "The room is loaded with guards." As to be expected. "Ansel's in a chair."

"The president?" Thea asked.

"He's about ready to do something. His body language seems skittish, though from the muffled words, I can tell he is talking coolly. Our presence has him scared. I think he knows his time is running out." Warren stood watching us all, his hand on his hips as he talked. The president should be scared and skittish. He should be afraid for what's to come because he had seen what we could do and now his life was like a ticking time bomb, ready to detonate.

"Our plan?" Thea asked as she stepped forward, her tiny frame straining on her tiptoes to peer into the window of the door.

"Our plan is—"

The floor shook underneath us as Thea's shadows rushed forward, bursting into the room. We hadn't had a plan. We hadn't discussed it. It was too late now, our presence was known, and Thea ... she was in front, leading us into a danger we had yet to assess. The shadows pulled from all corners of the room, pushing hard as the room engulfed in black. The screams of terror didn't faze her as she walked through the doors.

What had she seen to cause this? I knew, but she acted fast, taking the lead, doing what she had to in order to save her family. She really would make a good leader. A perfect one. There would never be a doubt in our country's future when it was led by a powerful lady with powerful men at her back. We stepped forward with her, the black hands of her shadows gripping onto the throats of guards and lifting them high in the air.

All eyes fell on her as she ended the life of men and, well, she was fucking terrifying. Life left them instantaneously, and the men who weren't at risk in her first round of fury had no chance in the second round. Her feet moved with purpose and we followed close behind her, each step feeling almost lighter than the previous one.

"You were going to use him as a lab rat. Again." She seethed.

President Brass took a step back, his body going behind Ansel's like a shield. His guards, mostly laid dead at his feet, but the men whose hands laid upon her mate? She kept alive, and I wondered, had they wished she would have killed them too? If they hadn't, they would. I guaranteed that much because there could be no good reason for Thea to keep those men alive unless she had further plans of pain.

She and Warren were too much alike. A perfect match. They didn't shy away from the torture of others. They didn't care that screams would echo off the ceiling as everything a person had done in their lifetime flashed in front of their eyes. What regrets did they have? Would this be one of them?

"He would have been fine. I think the dose is just right." The President's grin was definitely that of a man who had gone completely unhinged and was a professional at hiding the fact.

"These are lives you are playing with." Thea's voice cracked. "Our lives are not a game."

"Clearly." The President looked around, the men he paid to protect him littering the floor like garbage. "They had families, you know."

"So did we," she pointed out.

"About that. You'll never find your sister. Your mother was smart, you know. She had that child smuggled out before we realized it. But she won't escape again. You'll never find her. You'll find none of them."

I tried to ignore the tiny inhale of breath from Rodrick. The verbal confirmation that there was more, just like Thea, hidden throughout this country, was still a lot of information to handle. It was a dream, a dream we never thought would be true. And here we were, proof that omegas existed and that a chance at a real life was possible for us.

Thea's shadows crept forward. The edge of them glowed like embers and sparked tiny flames as they crept toward President Brass. His eyes grew wide, his movement swift as he grabbed onto Ansel's hair, threading his fingers in the strands as he yanked his head back, using the needle as a weapon against Ansel's jugular. The needle was so close to his skin that a single slip would pierce him.

"Put it down," Thea demanded.

"I think I'll keep it right where it's at." The President's eyes gleamed. "Tell me, Warren. What was it like to receive that second dose? Did it burn? Did you feel the very makeup of you altering and changing? Would you do it again?"

Warren didn't answer at first, but the threat of the needle close to Ansel's throat was too much to risk. "It felt like fire, everywhere. At first, the pain was dull, nothing I couldn't handle. But then I stood up. I made it three steps before the fire coursed through my veins. But I think you know this, since you were there. It lasted what seemed like hours, and when it was over, I was so weak I couldn't walk for days."

"You were weak, reacting so drastically."

"I was a child," Warren roared. "And I refuse to let my child suffer the same fate as I did."

"You think you have a choice? Who do you think is in control here? Who do you think will win in the end?" His fingers pulled tighter as he rubbed the needle against Ansel's neck.

He had the upper hand on us and barely. It wasn't that we couldn't win, because we could. We could destroy this very lab right this moment and all would be right in the world again. Except we weren't willing to risk Ansel in the process. Keeping him alive meant more to us than winning, and even if we lost this battle, we would win them eventually. Our men's power was equal to ten of theirs, or strategies far more superior. The President could stay in the lead, but it wouldn't last long.

"We won't back down." Thea's eyes burned. The red that I had seen in Warren's eyes swirled in her own. "Even if you kill us now, there is more. We will fight for the freedoms you had taken. You may leave here victorious, but that victory will be short."

"Look at you." The President laughed. "Have you forgotten that you were once on our side? Killing those people just like you, blindly following whatever truth and lie we fed you?"

"I hadn't forgotten. It's why I'm here. It won't happen again. I won't let anyone be manipulated as I had." She was moving closer, keeping him engaged and distracted while Ansel remained calm, his eyes staring off as if his life wasn't in danger.

"You think you were the only one? No. We've got many of you, so easy to manipulate, so desperate to fit in." Desperate to fit in? Maybe. But we were living things. We deserved so much more than fitting in. The President's hold on the needle shifted. "I wouldn't move if I were you."

Thea defiantly took a step closer; Warren and I close to her back. "Or what? Have you seen your guards?" Warren questioned. "Have you seen what a mated omega can do? Dead. The whole fucking lot of them, and for what? Power of a man whose only bargaining chip is a needle at a mutant's neck. Go ahead, finish him. Plunge it into his skin."

"Warren." Thea was alarmed at Warren's taunts, but if he was risking the life of one of our own, he had a reason.

"It's fine," Warren assured her. "It will be quick. Like a razor blade slicing through the skin."

What the fuck was he—

My eyes caught the glint of light that reflected off my belt buckle. The one that Ansel had apparently borrowed. I couldn't be more relieved at this moment to know that he wasn't as helpless as it seemed. He had something, and Warren was reminding him to use it. Just a single flick of his wrist. That was all it would take to release the weapon that was hidden inside of the belt buckle, just a tiny press of a button.

"Oh, Warren. If you remember correctly, it's a lot more than a quick slice. The pain that comes with this needle is unmatched. Would you like a reminder?"

"What is it you want, Brass? Really? Walking away isn't an option. At least not for all of us." Warren was losing patience, the reminder of his past only pushing him toward anger as smoke bellowed from his body.

"I want the child. After that, you can have your omega, do what you please with her. Promise me the child, and we all walk away. It's that simple."

It wasn't that simple, and he was delusional if he

thought so. Still, I had to trust in Warren's plan as he spoke. "Release Ansel in good faith, then."

"Only if you give me the omega," Brass demanded. "It's only temporary."

"Are we going to talk in circles?" Warren's smoke filled the room. The guards close to Ansel coughed and choked as it reached toward them. "You know you can't have my omega. The deal was for the child."

"Warren." Thea spoke again, but Warren held up his hand. "Silence. This isn't a conversation for a female."

I felt the ground rumble with Thea's anger, and I hoped she realized he was only playing into what the president wanted. He wanted Thea and the child—two things he would never give up. But if the doctor believed that Warren didn't find Thea as his equal, if he believed Thea didn't make her own decisions, he would bend, thinking Warren and his agendas aligned.

"I can't have the child without the omega. When the child is here... you can have her back."

"And I have your word?"

"Of course."

Warren looked at Thea. "Go ahead then, Thea, we've got a deal."

Chapter 18

THEA

A DEAL. We had a fucking deal? Fury pushed through every blood vessel in my body at the man I trusted to be my mate. The man who just traded me to the enemy for a member of his family that I apparently hadn't been a part of long enough to trump. I thought we were a team. A unit. We operated as one. But apparently that only counted if things were going his way.

I looked at him, his beautiful eyes gazing at me as if speaking without words. His tongue darted out, licking his lips before he nodded. "I said go ahead, Thea, we made a deal."

"No." My objection sounded weak. "You made a deal. I—"

"Will do as you're told, or I'll have him put you in chains."

Chains.

I wasn't a weak woman. But somehow the threat of

such an action hit differently coming from him. He would chain me. I could fight back, I fucking should. I could kill them all, mutant, man, the whole fucking lot of them. But the defeat and fight I had had vanished, vanished with the trust I had in Warren.

I let my eyes fall to Rex. "You can't let him do this."

"It's the only option, Thea. I promise."

He promised what? I wished I fucking knew. "You all are a lot of fucking bastards and I hope you rot in hell. You let me trust you. You fucking made me believe it."

Warren flinched, but there was no other emotion shown as he gestured me forward. I took a step and stopped before he pushed me toward the President of the United Government. If they thought they won, they were mistaken. I'd gather my strength, and I'd fight back, fight them every step of the fucking way. I'd do anything to protect this life that I wasn't even sure I wanted out of fucking principal. I wouldn't let them win.

I took the steps slowly. The President watched me with glee as Warren surrendered what he thought was his most prized possession. He was wrong. If I were the most prized possession, I wouldn't be taking these steps toward the enemy. Warren's most prized possession was his fucking ego, a thing so big and untouchable not a single soul can damage it, apparently.

My feet felt like lead, the heaviness making it hard to lift them up as they dragged against the floor. I couldn't focus on the danger in front of me, though I should. I was strong enough to bring them all down, take down the President whose smile taunted me and whose soulless eyes bored into me like I was the prize he'd always sought.

Five feet.

Four feet.

Three.

I'd kill Warren myself, after I saved Ansel. I'd pull his soul straight from his body and let him feel what it was like to die at the hands of darkness.

Two feet.

One...

Ansel's hand behind his back shot forward, reaching in front of his body and over so fast that it took me a moment to realize he had taken a dagger and drove it into the groin of the guard at his left. The guard fell fast, the howl of pain a temporary distraction that allowed Ansel to hit his belt. In seconds, a double edge blade released into his hand. The blade was hidden behind the larger decorative one. He jumped up, his swing slightly off as he blindly swung toward the President. The blade skimmed his cheek, blood instantly spouting down his face and onto the collar of his white shirt.

A single click was all Ansel needed before the President's throat was in his palm. A single click, to tell him that if he threw to the left, the President's body would crash into the remaining guards, who still hadn't lifted a finger to protect him. It was shock, it had to be. Because even this close to them, I was still glued in place, shocked at how fast the position of power had changed and shifted.

Warren stepped up close to me, his fingers sparking with rage as he went for the guard who was crying on the floor, the dagger still embedded into his body. He lifted the guard by his hair, pulling out the weapon as the guard's screams echoed off the building walls. His blood coated the floor as Warren took the dirty dagger and imbedded it in his throat, dragging the blade downward until his chest cavity was flayed open and his glassy eyes stared lifelessly.

His body dropped hard before Warren turned looking for the next victim. Only there weren't many guards left, most of them taken down when I first entered the room.

And the two that were left? They were cowering in the corner, terrified. The terror didn't matter to my men. Rex was on them while Warren cleaned off his weapon, wiping it on the shirt of the dead. Before I could blink, Rex had a knife impaled into one guard's skull. The other? He dragged by his hair to the middle of the room, dropping the man at my feet like an offering.

Rex's big eyes looked at me for approval, as one of his dimples appeared. Fuck, I adored him. The dimple was my weakness. I reached down for the guy, letting my shadows close in on us, surround us until we were locked in a bubble. His eyes bulged with fear as I pulled him up. His body shook uncontrollably. "Did you ever even care that you were on the wrong side of humanity?"

My question made him bat his eyes in confusion. "Wrong side? I get paid so I can feed my family. That's all that matters."

His voice was strong for a man who was about to die. "And what about my family?"

"H-he said mutants can't have families." He stuttered the words out.

"And yet, here we are. A family." Sort of, even though we were a fucking mess of one and I was still planning to stab Warren.

"But it's not real..." The guard spoke, degrading what we had created, the life we formed, and I didn't want to hear it. Science or not could go fuck itself. Scientifically, we shouldn't exist, but we do. Scientifically, we shouldn't be able to reproduce, but we had. Scientifically, our lives are not our own, but fuck the President, he didn't own us.

I let the shadows pull closer, squeezing against his skin, pushing into him as his pain morphed to unbearable heights. His screams were muffled by the bubble I formed around us and when his skull split open, popped in half by the pressure the shadows put on it, the gore spattered against the shadows and slid down them like glass, landing in a neat puddle on the floor.

I let the shadows snap back in place, disappearing from around me, giving me a view of my surroundings. The guards were all dead, and my boys? They were cornering the President, even as he stood his ground, his precious needle in hand and blood dripping down his face.

"We can work this out," he offered.

But no deal with him would be worth letting him live. Warren's chest puffed up. "We could have worked this out years ago. Now? Now it's too late for you. It's too late for all of us."

"You have to realize the sacrifices you made were for the good of humanity," President Brass tried to explain.

"Humanity was never lacking in strength, only guidance." Ansel stood there, his frame hovering over the country's leader.

"I-I can help guide."

Warren laughed at that; the sound rich with amusement. "Help. Like you've helped since the government rebuilt. You made it worse; you made it into your own personal agenda. We are equals. Why aren't we treated as such?"

"Equals?" The President repeated the words as if it was foreign on his tongue. "It's impossible—"

His sentence was cut short by a sudden moan as Warren's clawed fingers swiped forward, tearing into his abdomen. He lifted him up; the blood flowing down Warren's arms as he held him in the air. "It was impossible to treat us how we deserved. It was never impossible to reject the urge to alter who a person is. It was never impossible to let a child be a child." I heard a snap, and I knew Warren had broken his spine, rendering him immobile as he tossed him to the ground, hovering over him as he examined him in disgust. "It was never impossible to be human."

Warren's eyes fell on me. "Finish him." Finish him? He was already on his way to death. "Take what he had taken from you."

Taken from me? What he took from me was my life, but his was already fading. He took my family, but I had built a new one. He took the very person I was and morphed it into what I was now. He took my very soul and altered it and ...

And I'd take his in return.

I stepped forward, closing my eyes in concentration as I tried to center myself. If Warren could do it, so could I. Hadn't that been proven so many times before in a short few weeks we'd been in each other's lives? Weeks? Had it only been weeks? Yet, look what we'd accomplished. Mutation was a funny thing. We thought we had no opportunities, and yet, all we had lying in front of us were opportunities. Freedoms. Anything we desired was ours for the taking.

I bit my lip as I inhaled, feeling the pull Warren so often talked about, letting it connect with my body as whimpers and screams of pain increased. My mouth opened, doing so against my control. It was an odd feeling; one I doubted I could ever replicate. But as I inhaled, I felt strands leave my body, and when they all reached the end, the teether pulled them back, dragging them through the air as it carried a heaviness toward me. The soul entered my mouth and slid down my throat like jelly but settled in my stomach like heavy marble.

I was horrified. Ashamed. Nauseous. When the soul settled, and I looked down, I nearly fainted as the blank eyes looked back at me. This wasn't me. I was never this weak. I killed, brutally and professionally, for most of my adult life. But taking a soul into me... letting it reside inside of my body and become one with me was way more intimate than I had thought.

I swallowed hard and turned, looking toward my men who stood in puddles of red spilled onto the stark tiles. Their eyes were wide as they watched me, but it was Warren who held a hand out toward me, gentling his tone as he spoke. "It's okay, Thea. You won't feel it long."

Impossible. The feeling of a soul shifting inside of me will always be there. I'd never escape it; I wasn't sure if I wanted to. I didn't understand how he could do it so freely, steal the very makeup of a person, and still be so very gentle with me. It made little sense. My mind couldn't compute the contrast.

"I—" I tried, by my mind grew dizzy. I stumbled, Rex catching me before I fell. "I don't know what happened."

I got the words out as my vision blanked. My sight was tunneling, my head swirling, and right before the blackness took over, I heard Rodrick say, "I'd seen nothing like that before. She's... she's..."

"She's all fucking mine," Warren growled and then the world went black.

Chapter 19

WARREN

SHE STOOD ON THE PODIUM, addressing the crowd of people. And I'd never been more fucking proud of a person in my entire life. Her speech was flawless, a perfect mix of her and Ansel. Her demeanor, though nervous, showed the unmistakable signs of coaching by Rex, who can please any crowd with a charming smile and witty conversation. As for me? Well, I had been perfectly content to sit back and watch my family rebuild a society that was unfairly broken by its leader and add my opinion when asked.

It was never asked. Not by Thea, at least. My love was still angry at my attempt to turn her over, but she had to know I would never do it. I couldn't. I just needed to give Ansel the distraction he needed to release the blade from Rex's buckle and catch the President off guard. I would die before I handed her over to the enemy, but I couldn't tell her that. She wouldn't hear any of it, not with her giving me the cold shoulder.

"We cannot promise that this country will be perfect right from the start." Her voice boomed over the crowd. "But we can promise that each day that passes, we'll work our way toward more peace, more equality, and more unity than we've seen in years. We can do it together."

The crowd applauded, though I noted a few humans lining the back who watched on with scowls on their face and didn't raise their hand in applause. I'd watch them close and if we didn't win them over, if they became a threat of any kind, I'd deal with them personally. That was what I was here for now, the muscle and protection around Thea. Unanimously, our group picked her to led us. Because none of us could lead a country and keep her protected. We wouldn't be able to divide our attention. We wouldn't have been able to do much but worry about her.

A low-level mutant raised his hand and Rex pointed at him, giving him the opportunity to ask his question. "My sister, she was taken. I know she wasn't the first one. I'd heard rumors, a lot of them were. Can we, I mean, are there records we can access to find her? She ain't done nothing wrong, I swear it. One minute she was on the porch, enjoying the weather, the next, they came and snatched her."

Thea cleared her throat and looked at Rex for reassurance. Rex, not me. She refused to fucking look at me. Her tongue darted out to moisten her lips before she spoke. "We are aware of this travesty. I, too, have had a family member fall victim to former President Brass's collections. We are currently looking into the whereabouts of the facilities holding these innocent members of society and building a team designed to release them back to society."

The same man raised his hand again and Rex nodded,

giving his approval for him to speak. "I- I... I would like to help. Please. I mean, I volunteer. Can I do that? Volunteer to be on a team? I want to do my part. This is my family."

It was his family. It was all of our families. We were all one now, a group of individuals linked by the tragic abuse of power and knowledge. Rex looked at me and I gave him a slight nod. We needed people. We needed support. We needed freedom. With a slight nod from Rex to Thea, she spoke again. "If you would like to volunteer to find your family and others, we would gladly take your support."

With that statement, though it was directed at a single person, caused hands to shoot up rapidly. Each time Rex pointed at someone, all they said was, "I volunteer."

My heart swelled watching it. Both human and mutant were not ashamed to admit that they supported a movement of salvation, a luxury they had been deprived of for so many fucking years. Thea's voice cracked for a moment, then grew stronger. "We will put out a sign up at the end of this conference. If you wish to volunteer, please provide us with your name and contact informa-tion. But it's important to understand, and I can not stress this enough, that this is a team to find and rescue our families. There is no room in our new foundation for hatred of any kind. We, as mutant, love our fellow mutants, but that does not hinder our love for the unscathed human. They have been misdirected in their leadership and I ask that we offer them grace for what they had never experienced. We educate them on our misfortunes because this was not our choice. The right to live normally was stolen and now we will live normally as equals."

More clapping and some cheers, a good sign that we were doing something correct. Thea bit her lip, the only sign that she was nervous. "All other questions can be left with the sign-up sheet and we'll work to answer it at a further date."

With a nod to the crowd, she turned and walked away from the podium, then down the three steps of the stage. Her steps increased as she walked toward the door, a room away from the crowds of people who wanted answers and expectations from the leader of a newly developing government. It was a lot of pressure, but I knew that with our help, our omega could handle it. She was strong. Fierce. And so fucking sexy I could barely keep my hands off her.

In front of us, Rodrick held the door, waiting for Thea to come through before locking the world out. When we stepped through, the door slammed shut. Thea turned, her face red, and she twisted her fingers together. "That went better than I thought."

"There were some people that I saw did not agree with this new formation. We need to keep our guard up. The best time to uprise is when a government is already fragile. We are new, learning, forming, there could be trouble."

"Let it come," Rodrick stated. "We've been preparing for this for years."

"I'd like to avoid it at all costs," Rex stated. "Thea is fragile right now."

That was another layer of complications we hadn't yet discussed. We would, of course... but not now. It wasn't as important at this moment. At the moment, the only thing of importance is that Thea fucking forgives me instead of this cold shoulder bullshit. Was she acting immature? Hormonal? Insane? Absolutely. Was I going to fucking say that to her? I sure as fuck wouldn't.

"I have men out there collecting names and contact information." Rodrick looked at us all. "I didn't predict that as an outcome."

"Neither did I, but I'd welcome it. Monitor the men

that lined the back wall. They didn't seem as thrilled about the takeover as others." My brows pulled together, thinking about the looks on their face as they watched Thea. "See that they're followed."

"Already done," Rodrick confirmed. "Nothing is going to stop this reform, Warren. Nothing will stop us."

"I don't plan on letting anything halt our progress," I stated as I stared at Thea, willing her to say something to me. Something at all. When she didn't speak, I did. "Everyone but Thea out. Now."

"We need to discuss..." Ansel began.

"I said, out!" The roar of my voice shook the doors on the hinges, but it got the point across.

Rex leaned in and kissed Thea's cheek, while whispering his apologies while she called him a traitor. Ansel didn't bother with guilt. He knew exactly why I wanted to be alone in this room and he would not come between us. The boys left, Rodrick taking up the rear before closing it. I walked after him, clicking the lock in place, the sound booming in the silence. I turned on my heals, crossed my arm and stared at her, waiting.

When the presence of my eyes against her skin became too much, she sneered. "What?"

"We clearly need to talk."

"Clearly to whom?"

"You're vexed with me," I pointed out.

"Assumptions. You always have them." She rolled her eyes.

"You're not angry at Ansel and Rex." It was true; it was only me whom she directed her anger at.

"It's because they came to me and talked. You? No. You expect that because you carry around your macho energy, I'm to just accept all that you say."

"Have I offended you, Thea? Do I owe you an apology?"

She sat down on the edge of the desk, the curves of her body looking absolutely delicious. Did she realize already she was changing? New curves were forming, enticing the dragon inside of me. I breathed out a puff of air, smoke rising from the breath. He always wanted to come out and play with her around, and keeping him contained was nearly impossible. He was obsessed, wanting to be near her at all moments of the day.

Her throat bobbed as I took a step toward her. I knew she couldn't resist me forever. Our pull was too fucking great. But damn it, my stubborn omega was going to fucking try her hardest to stay mad. "You were going to just give me up."

"I think we both know that was never a real option."

"But if Ansel wasn't successful at taking him off guard? You put faith that Ansel understood what you intended, and I was your bait."

"The thing is, Thea, I don't think this is why you're really mad. Is it?" I stepped closer, standing so close to her I could feel the heat radiating off her body. This close, her scent, apple pie, made my cock hard as a fucking rock. It had been too long, too fucking long, since I'd been inside her body.

Her back stiffened, her posture telling me she was on guard. She wanted to cave to me, but I knew she would make me work for it, at least a little. "I don't know what you're talking about, Warren."

I let my hand come up, a single finger tapping her chin. "I think you do."

She pulled away from my touch. "No."

"I think you're scared, Thea."

She shook her head vigorously, only confirming my suspicion. "No."

"Yes. Only, the question is, of what?"

"You tried to trade me, Warren. Is that not enough?"

My fingers reached up to grasp a lock of hair, twirling it around my finger. In an instant, the sharp edge of a letter opener was pressed against my stomach. My tongue darted out, rubbing against my upper lip as my eyes roamed over her. "I think we both know that I don't cave to threats, omega. If you're going to stab me, do it already. I've been waiting since the day I've met you to have my blood coat your skin like yours coated mine when I devoured you."

Her cheeks reddened. "You don't think I'll do it?"

"Oh, darling, I know you would. I'm begging you not to hesitate." When she didn't plunge the sharp edge into my skin, I let my hands fall between us, cupping her tiny fingers in mine as I forced the letter opener from her hand. I tossed it onto the desk before I buried my palm into the hair at the nape of her neck. "Now tell me, what do I need to apologize for?"

Her enormous eyes looked up at me, seeing into my soul. But she didn't answer me as she looked on defiantly, daring me to cross her. I would never. She should know that.

"Is it because of what happened at Rodrick's place? Do you regret what we had done?"

I hoped she said no. I wouldn't be able to handle myself if my omega regretted growing our family. It was my dream, all of our dreams. She gave us what should be impossible. It was a gift. She was a fucking gift.

Her eyes wielded with tears, and inside, I panicked. Thea wasn't a crier. She would more than likely kill you instead of showing an emotion like that. "It's your fault."

If it made her stop crying, I'd take the responsibility. "Of course it is, Doe." Only I didn't know what the fuck I did. "Mind if I ask what I did?"

"I… the souls. I can't get the feeling of it sloshing inside of me out of my mind. I feel like it's always there. Under my skin. It's disgusting." Her whole body shivered at the confession.

"And you blame me?" I clarified.

"Why wouldn't I? I never had that ability until you… you…"

She stuttered, so I finished for her. "Mated the most attractive woman out there?"

"Don't flatter me, Warren. I'm angry at you."

She was angry at me. I could tell by the sight of faint strands of smoke that rose from her body without her knowing. I tried to fight the grin. I truly did. But it was nearly impossible when I could see all the clear signs that we were one. She was a part of me for fucking ever now and I'd like to hear her disputes about that fact as she displays my mutational traits like a badge of ownership.

I leaned down, kissing her forehead. "Doe. We had no way of knowing that would happen when we mated."

"You could have guessed. You fucking guessed about everything else." The words held venom, a contrast to her hands that had gripped my shirt tightly, like she was afraid to let go.

"Think of it this way: any part of us you've absorbed will only make you that much stronger for our child. Like the ultimate mama mutant." I smiled widely, proud of my play on the outdated term of the past when mothers once called themselves mama bears.

Her eyes grew wide at the mention of our child. "That's another thing..."

I didn't give time for her to chew me out like I knew

she was going to. We did not ask permission of her to be a carrier, and I knew that. I ignorantly thought it was clear, and well, I knew she wasn't thrilled about the latest development. Before she could object about it, I crashed my lips to hers, forcing her body to lean hard into the desk behind her.

Her hand pushed at my chest, and I pulled away. "You're trying to distract me."

"I am," I admitted as I chased her lips again. Our lips met effortlessly. She could pretend all she wanted, but I knew there wasn't any real fight in her, not the way her lips gave against my assault.

Thea pulled away again, gave my lips a quick peck, before reminding me, "I'm still mad."

She crossed her arms in front of herself like a shield, and I instantly took her hands and pulled them to her sides. I'd not have her shield herself from me. "Then let me remind you of all the reasons you love us."

"I don't love you," she declared.

I leaned down and kissed her neck. "Always such a liar." She held her back straight, but her body was melting into me. "Still mad?"

Her eyes blinked a few times and I could tell that she was fighting the emotions of whatever she felt. "I'm..."

"You can talk to me, Thea." I snaked my hand up her thigh, slipping under the tight knee-length skirt she wore. "Always."

Her throat bobbed, but her legs parted to allow me room. She leaned more into the desk, stabilizing her weight against the solid piece of furniture. "I'm not mad. I mean, yes, I'm angry, because I don't know how to feel about this all and the souls... that's just... it's awful, Warren, it really is."

"But?" My hands found the edge of her panties and I skimmed along the edge of them.

Her breath quickened as she spoke, the words breaking as they left her mouth. "I'm scared."

I froze. Never in my life did I think my knife wielding, men slaughtering, feisty wisp of a mate would admit to such things. But she had, and I didn't know what to do with the information. My heart pounded as I asked, "Of what, Doe? Tell me what you fear."

I couldn't bring myself to move. I was afraid to breathe. Whatever she had to say was important to her, worried her, made my fierce woman vulnerable, and I needed to listen and absorb all of those worries so the fear was no longer hers, but ours. Her fingers gripped into the wood of the desk and I heard it give with a slight crack as she dented it. Strength, another thing that had become new to her, another thing she had gotten from me. And I knew she hated it, but fuck, I was proud.

She looked at the floor as she spoke, and I refused to let that continue; I forced her eyes up, locking them with my own. "I'm scared of this, all of this. The souls I consumed. The strength. Being mated... the... the..." She gestured to her stomach. "What ramifications will all this have on it? And ruling this country? I don't know what I'm fucking doing, and we're going to fuck this kid up."

"Most definitely," I agreed, and her eyes went wild with panic, but I stopped her. "We're definitely going to fuck a lot of shit up, but we'd do it together. If we all go down, it's as one, Thea. Haven't you learned that by now? It may seem that it's all a solo journey, but it isn't. It's a journey bigger than you and I. Bigger than the four of us. We've got all the help we could need. We just have to extend our hands and reach for it."

"I don't know how."

Of course she didn't. She spent her whole life fighting the world, living, and navigating it by herself. The one person who she looked up to was the same man who had been working for our enemy the entire time. She couldn't just trust people, not when her trust had been betrayed, and she was so damn used to being independent.

"If you don't know how, I'll show you." I picked her up and turned her around, trailing my fingers down her arms before threading our fingers together. I placed our locked palms onto the desk in front of us as my body hunched over hers. " First step—trust and follow the orders of your alpha"

She swallowed hard. "Never..."

I bit down into the skin on her shoulder. "Then I'll have to fuck you into obedience."

"I'd like to see you try." She gasped as my tongue skimmed over the shell of her ear.

I tugged her earlobe into my teeth. "Challenge accepted."

Chapter 20

THEA

CHALLENGE ACCEPTED.

His words rang through my mind, but I hadn't fully processed the meaning of them until the hard length of his cock was snug against my ass. I wanted to be angry, to hate him and blame him because so many things had changed in my life because of him, and I wasn't ready to fully process all the chances. I didn't think anyone with a sound mind could.

"I don't want your hands to move from the desk. Do you understand me?" he commanded as his knee pushed between my thighs, forcing my legs to open wider. His palms crushed against my fingers as he demanded I not move.

"I thought I was in charge here." My words came out breathlessly; my anticipation clear.

"In front of our nation, Doe... you can lead me around by a collar and claim your ownership. But behind closed doors? I own every inch of you and I'm never going to relinquish control of it."

His words made my stomach tighten with anticipation. "I'm still not happy with you."

"Then I'll make you happy."

"You don't get to decide that." My nails bit into the wood as his fingers traveled down my body, brushing against the skin and clothing as he freed my body of the fabric I wore.

"You're right, I don't." His fingers snagged my under-wear as he pulled my skirt down, tearing the material away from my body. "But when you're screaming my name, begging for me, there's no fucking possible way you could be sad. You'll do that for me, won't you, Doe? Scream my name?"

His mouth was so close to my ear when he whispered his question—or was it a demand—that I could feel his breath tickle against my skin. My pulse raced, my core flooded, and though he hadn't really touched me besides a few roaming hands and skimming fingers, my body tensed and prepared to release.

I turned my head, trying to look at him even though he was behind me. When our eyes locked, I pushed the words out, "Make me."

As if making me scream his name was the biggest chal-lenge ever issued, his eyes went feral before he pulled his body away from my back. The sound of his belt being unlaced and the material of his pants hitting the floor was the only sign that he had heard me at all.

When I thought that time had stopped and the silence would suffocate me, stealing all air from my lungs until they burned with the need to breathe and speak, to break the surrounding bubble, Warren's palm landed on my back again. His voice was rough, scratched with the torture of maintaining control as he spoke. "Make you. Doe, I'm going to have you screaming my name so loud that there will be no fucking doubt who is really in charge of this desolate country."

I didn't have time to reply. I didn't have a moment to let a snarky word fall from my lips that I knew damn well would only goad him. Before I could even utter a sigh or fully take in a breath of air, his fingers grabbed onto my hips, digging into my skin with a bruising intensity, before he pushed himself into my body. The intrusion made me gasp. His size was always a surprise, even if it was welcoming.

He leaned down again as a single hand ran up my back and stopped at my hair. His fists wound into the strands as he used the grip to pull my body back, forcing my spine to arch toward him. "Are you fucking ready, Doe?"

I could feel his cock pulsing inside of me, a gentle throb as he fought to not move, and with each pulse, my body clenched savoring the feel of the movement. "Make me."

"Keep your fingers on the fucking desk," he demanded as he pulled out, plunging his body back into me hard enough that I jolted forward. The single movement, just the one, was enough to make my eyes nearly roll. The plea-sure so fucking intense that I was sure I might die from it. And just when the jolts of pleasure from that one action faded, he did it again. Over and over again. Repeatedly. Until every cell in my body screamed with lust and the need to cum. And the only name I could think of was his.

But I wouldn't scream it.

I wouldn't give him the satisfaction.

His palm pushed down on my skull, forcing my head to bend until my cheek met the cold wood of the desk. "Ready to scream my name, Thea?"

"You'd have to be..." I had to pause because my body was so fucking worked up I could hardly breathe. "Something special first."

He leaned down, his palm grinding harder into my hair as he spoke next to my cheek. "You want something special?"

"Extraordinary," I gasped.

"I'm not sweet like Rex."

Fuck. Had he always been so large, or was that a recent development? Had my nerves always been this sensitive?

"I'm don't think ahead like Ansel."

I bit my lip on a gasp before I spoke. "I never asked you to be anything like them."

"Good." His face shot forward close to mine, and before I could even process what had happened, he had nipped at my cheek. The pain was nothing compared to the pain that suddenly struck through my shoulder. His teeth dug into my skin, piercing it effortlessly. He pulled away. "I'm not nice, Thea. And I always get what I want. It's best you know that now."

I'd known it. I'd known it from the moment I glimpsed him for the first time, while he had me tied up to a chair in his warehouse. I'd known it, and I fought it because what he wanted was me, and that was the one thing I never wanted to give up. But now? Fuck, he owned me. I'd never say those words out loud; I'd never give him the satisfaction.

"And you want?"

"My fucking name from those lips, Thea. I want you to vibrate this entire room with the sound of your screams. I want to hear you gasp your pleas and beg me to let up from the relentlessness of my cock slamming inside of you." My fingers curled into the wood at his words, taking some varnish with them. A low rumble of satisfaction shook his chest as his fingers pulled my hair. "I want you, my mate, to give it all to me."

"Never." It was a lie and we both fucking knew it. I was so close to losing it, so close to exploding, that I could barely hold my own body weight. Even with the desk under me for support and Warren's powerful hands against my skin, I felt weak.

He paused, his cock stopping its movement for a moment. The moment stretched on, feeling like a prison of infinity. His hand reached forward, his skin gone as he fought his dragon, the skeletal bones left in his place. He wrapped his hand around my neck tightly, pulling me back toward him. He forced me to stand, allowing me no room to move as he trapped me against the desk and his body. "Never?"

"Never," I whispered the words, then felt his hand against my throat, suffocating and liberating me.

Without another word, heat burned into the skin of my neck as his hips sped up. He slammed his body into mine hard, forcing the desk forward with each thrust as the heat he forced into my body slowly traveled downward, consuming every limb, every vein, every nerve, until it reached my stomach.

My body tensed. The feeling of his relentless cock and the fire he ignited inside of me was nearly too much for me to take. "Scream it, Thea."

His voice was soft against my skin, nearly a plea for him to get what he wanted. "Make me."

In this moment, that was the worst thing I could have ever said to a double mutated, half man, half dragon, with control issues. His grip on my neck tightened, stealing my air as he pushed the fire the last inches to my core. The heat hit my clit and pulled, manipulating it without Warren placing a single finger against it, and I fought it. I truly did.

But with him buried deep in me, and the heat pulling at my clit, I was losing control.

My body clenched and Warren cursed before he spoke in my ear. "Scream it, Thea. Let them know who is fucking you so hard that you've lost all control."

Before I could dispute it and deny him, his cock pounded into my channel, hard and fast. The knot swelled, and it set my nerves blazing. I wanted to pull away; the feeling was too fucking much, too intense to handle, but his hand against my throat forced me to stay in place, forced me to take all he was giving me until my body pulsed and squeezed around him... and his name did indeed fall from my lips loud enough to have people pounding on the locked door, begging to get inside. I couldn't bring myself to care or be embarrassed. Not when my body felt so fucking alive with pleasure that my lungs forgot to work and my heart nearly stopped beating.

"Breathe, Thea," Warren whispered, and I gasped, taking in some much-needed air into my lungs. "Good girl."

The coo of his praise was cut off by a low rumble of his chest before his knot swelled, forcing another wave of pleasure out of me as his cum spurted inside my body. My vision faded, my body shook, and when my orgasm ebbed and I could finally breathe again, I spoke.

"I fucking hate you, Warren."

His palm rubbed lovingly through my hair as the sound of the lock clicking open from the door echoed. His body was still locked inside of me, his knot refusing to let us separate. "You said I fucking hate that I love you, Warren."

I fucking hated that he was right.

Chapter 21

REX

THEA SAT at the head of the table. To her left, I sat. To her right, Ansel. And if your gaze followed you to the opposite end, Warren sat, commanding the group equally. Our unit, our group, our family, was something fierce and nothing to be fucked with. Warren and Thea had proven as much.

"The list." Rodrick's voice boomed. "Rex. We need the list."

Fuck, how long had they been calling me? Talking to me? Discussing the thing I had in my very hand while I spaced out, staring at my mate like I could and would devour her on this very table. I leaned forward, the chair squeaking loudly as I tossed the papers into the center of the table for Rodrick to grab.

He leaned over and scooped them up, reviewing the notes I had left, and reading through my summary. A low whistle escaped his lips. "That's a lot of men."

"There are a lot of women missing," I pointed out.

"Do you trust all those who volunteered?" Warren's fingers steepled in front of him as he leaned forward, his eyes on Thea as he smirked, no doubt remembering the position I caught them in a few hours prior.

My face flamed as I thought of the two, my family, locked together over the desk. "I don't know them well enough to trust them. We need a vetting process. Interviews. Maybe various levels of clearances."

Thea addressed Rodrick. "Can you organize that?"

"We're already on it, omega." He smiled at Thea, goading Warren with his fake infatuation.

"Are you though?" she questioned.

His smile faltered for a moment. "We will be."

She gave him an unamused look. "I trust you because Warren trusts you. That doesn't mean I won't stab you."

Rodrick's face flushed as he looked toward Thea, then Warren, then the rest of the table. "I swear to whatever power is in this universe, if you don't guard this omega, I will be the one to take her from you."

The table cracked under the weight of Warren as he stood, his palms flat on the wood as smoke rose and the smell of burned tinder filled our conference room. "You will not touch my omega."

"I mean, I might," Rodrick taunted, too dumb to know when to stop. "If it becomes clear that you can't satisfy her yourself."

"My mate is always satisfied," Warren declared, a thin layer of fire coating his skin as it altered from flesh to bone.

I stepped in, breaking up the conversation before Warren's dragon surfaced. "We all heard how satisfied she could be. Can we focus, please? We need at least some plans made before we exit this room or we will be in here forever."

Ansel leaned forward, his eyes blinking a few times. I wondered, even if he never admitted it fully, that if Warren and Thea can channel each other's ability, had he been able to get glimpses of vision? Was it possible? Improving each moment until it was restored in full? A dream, a hope, something for us to work toward as we grow together. His throat cleared, his face a mask as he pushed away whatever was distracting him. "I'll help vet them. I can hear the heartbeat when I'm close. They can lie to you, but can their heart lie?"

"Smart," Warren replied as he sat down, still glaring at Rodrick. "Thea, I have some friends over the next few weeks I'd like to bring in for you to meet."

"I'd rather not," she muttered.

"It won't be that bad," I assured her.

"Listen, I never asked for this. It's all more than I can handle right now." She leaned back, suddenly looking exhausted. How fucking selfish were we to neglect the fact that our mate needed more rest than normal?

"You're doing amazing," I assured her. "The people Warren wants to bring in will help make the jobs easier. We've been planning this for a while now, Thea. Everyone has their part. It won't be like the governments we left behind. It will be so much stronger."

"Can you guarantee that?" She leaned forward, her elbows on the table as she used it to support some of her weight.

"Can we guarantee it?" Warren responded. "No. But I can promise you I'd never put your life at risk willingly. The men I have lined up, both mutant and man, it will make this country stronger than before."

"Man?"

"I told you, Thea, I wanted equality. That was all. Equality wasn't something we were offered previously. Now? Now we control how equal this country will be, and any rights one person gets, we all do." His eyes burned as he looked around the room. The red of the fire he held hidden inside of him rimmed his irises. "Is that clear to everyone? We play no favoritisms. We protect the good, the man, the woman, the child, the mutants. Anyone who opposes that would willingly be stepping to their death and destruction. Do I make myself clear?"

Everyone nodded, and a few hums of approval filled the air. With that out of the way, it left us with room to discuss the basic foundation of the upcoming plans. There were conferences, interviews, laws to toss out, laws to make, and all of it was too much for my head to manage. I zoned out halfway through the meeting and I didn't snap back into it until everyone collected their things and chairs scraped against the floor. I jolted to attention and stretched. I knew I missed a lot. But fuck, did they really expect me to focus that long? I'd look at the notes from the meeting later.

Everyone was just about ready to stand when Thea stopped them. "One more thing." Movement paused as everyone waited for her to speak. "I'd like Bethany found."

"Thea, you know we are looking for the locations of facilities, but everything is so cryptic," Ansel commented.

"I understand. But she is family, my family, and well..."

"She's ours," Warren reassured her. "If she is family to you, she is family to us all."

Thea cleared her throat. "I appreciate it. But I want Rodrick's team specifically after her. That's his top priority. The other rescues are important. I know this, and I would never stop or hinder any of it. But when it comes to Bethany, I need to know she's in the best hands. Will you do that for me, Rodrick? Will you bring my sister home?"

The room was deafeningly silent as all eyes were on Rodrick, waiting for him to respond. It was an enormous responsibility. We all were fucking aware of that. But it meant the world that Thea, who trusted no one, will trust him with one of the most important people in her life. And Rodrick? Well, I wasn't playing matchmaker, but another omega could change things around here. Women were the foundation of a family, and the more we had under our wings, the greater of a family, of a country, we would have.

Plus, I met the omega, even though it was a brief encounter, and I knew she would give Rodrick hell. All the men, really. And I can verify that hell from an omega is damn near impossible to pass up. It was our kryptonite. A weakness. One little taste and we were damn near begging for more.

Rodrick shifted in his chair; his notes clutched so tight in his hands that for a moment I suspected he would tear right through the notebook. I understood it was a hard promise to make, a vow a man here wouldn't take lightly. A request as personal as that from the new ruler of our free country, and it was directed right at him. When I thought he wouldn't answer, he stood, his body bowed slightly before he spoke. "It would be my honor to bring home a member of your family and part of our team, Thea. We will start mining for intel right away."

He turned on his heals fast and was out of the room before anyone could say another word. The remaining people gathered the rest of their belongings and followed him, leaving us alone in the conference room. When the door slammed shut, Warren pulled Thea into his lap. His nose nuzzled against her, and I didn't miss the deep breath he took in as he seeked comfort in her scent. "You know, we could get her for you. She would be safe with us. You know that, right?"

A wicked smile curled her lips. "I know, but where's the fun in that?"

THANK YOU FOR READING!

Like what you read? I would love if you left a review!
Feel like hanging out with me?
Check out my Facebook reader's group, Delilah's Darlings.
Want the latest updates?
Visit me on Facebook at https://www.facebook.com/delilahmohan/
Website:
Delilahmohan.com
Sign up for my Newsletter here!

-
-
Other works by Delilah Mohan
-
PARANORMAL ROMANCE/ REVERSE HAREM
Claiming Claire (A reverse harem shifter novella)
Saving a Succubus
Training A Succubus
Liberty (Keeping Liberty Series)
Justice (Keeping Liberty Series)
Truth (Keeping Liberty Series)
Retribution (Keeping Liberty Series)
Resisted (Wolves of Full Moon Bay book 1)
Refused (Wolves of Full Moon Bay book 2)

Redeemed (Wolves of full moon bay 3)
UMBRA (With the Shadows 1)
BLAZE (With the Shadows 2)
SONDER (With the Shadows 3) Winter '23
Heidi and the Haunters

-

-

CONTEMPORARY ROMANCE
Obscured Love (Obscured Love Series, book 1)
Eluding Fate
Ricochet (Obscured Love Series, book 2)
Five Seconds to Love (Obscured Love Series, book 3)

Resisting Royal (The Repayment Series, book 1)
Owning Emma (The Repayment Series, book 2)
Salvaged Girl
Saints of Sin

Made in the USA
Monee, IL
18 April 2024

56860671R00114